Interview with a Psychic Assassin

A novel by

Inelia Benz

Also by Inelia Benz
Interview with an Alien

Published by Ascension Publishing Inc. 2014

Author contact details:
www.inelia.com

Cover by: Cristina Pandia and Augustin Georgescu

First Printing: 2015

ISBN: 978-1-312-79497-9

Disclaimer

This is a work of fiction.

Names, character, places and incidents either are products of the author's imagination or are used fictitiously. Any resemblance to actual events or locales or persons, living or dead is entirely coincidental.

Acknowledgments

I would like to thank Ilie Pandia for making the editing, finishing, publishing and distribution of this book possible. Lance White for your incredibly gifted proofreading and editing skills. Larry Buzzell whose unconditional love, support, delicious meals, and editing suggestions made the book what it is today. You are my three angels guys! And I love you more than words can express.

Thank you also to my brother Alex who did the final book revision and for all the guys and gals at Walk With Me Now, with whom all journeys are made into extraordinary experiences.

Table of Contents

Introduction

In 2009 I wrote the now very popular *Interview With An Alien* book. Since then, my friend whom I had interviewed in the book, moved away to a different location and continued her anonymous work among us.

Two months ago, she sent me a note. It was stuck to my front door when I got home from the store. It said:

"My Dearest Inelia,

As you know, contacting you by electronic or traceable ways is no longer possible. I knew this would be the case when we first decided to do the interview. I told you then that I would help you write more books, and that is why I am sending you this urgent note.

There is a woman I want you to meet. What she has to say, what she represents, and the information she wants to share, is very relevant for the Earth today.

Her name is Ramona, and she is what you might call a "psychic assassin".

No need to let me know what you decide to do, I will know your answer and so will Ramona. If you decide to do this interview, she will be in touch.

I love you dearly, and I know we will be able to meet again openly without danger of either of our paths being derailed by external circumstances or intentions.

Your friend."

I read the note over and over, looking and tapping into the energies contained within. I could feel my friend's energy and love in the note, along with the energy of several individuals that had carried the note across what appeared to be several countries, finally to the person who had stuck it on my front door.

I wanted to reach out to my friend and tell her how right she was about me giving seminars and retreats on the topic of Ascension. It was something that was totally off key and impossible for me to see in 2009. I wanted to tell her so many things.

Then I felt Ramona. Her energy was like black transparent glass - vast like the night sky, yet filled with stars. It was also very feminine, and youthful. She reminded me of an innocent little girl filled with rage and anger. I saw a visual of what she looked like: small, black hair, brown skin, big eyes, thin lips and nose, all delicate features like fine porcelain. She sent me a greeting and expectation of response.

Immediately I replied, "yes."

This book was began in the traditional interview style, as a series of questions and answers. However, the interview ended dramatically before we were done, and what followed was an adventure the likes of which I had never experienced before.

And now the disclaimer:

THIS BOOK IS A WORK OF FICTION.

Chapter One: First Interview

The airline ticket arrived via regular post. This surprised me because I hadn't had any contact from Ramona in any way since the initial introduction we had when I received the note from my friend.

It was a one week round trip ticket to Costa Rica during a week that had mysteriously cleared up in my calendar overnight, including a stay at a 5 star hotel. I had three days to pack.

My flight to Costa Rica went without incident. I mentioned it to my subscribers at ascension101, and the public at large, but didn't give many details, such as the final destination, when I was going to arrive, or that I was meeting Ramona.

A driver from the hotel was waiting for me at Daniel Oduber International Airport, in Liberia. I was pleasantly surprised at his energy field, friendliness, manners and openness. When I arrived at the hotel, the staff was also amazingly open and friendly. This was a good start to my "holiday".

I knew Ramona would not be there to greet me. She had allowed me time to settle into the place and the new energies. She would be arriving at the hotel the next day and the staff told me she would meet me for lunch.

I spent the next morning swimming in the sea, and eating amazing freshly picked live fruits.

I was very excited about meeting Ramona. There was something about her that made me feel as if I was meeting someone I already knew. At noon, I walked down to the hotel restaurant, and set myself up with my audio recorders, paper notebook, pens, and laptop.

Deep in my own thoughts, I didn't sense Ramona enter the room, nor did I realize she was there until she was standing right in front of me, with a wide smile and her hand extended.

We shook hands, an odd way to greet another woman in South America, and exchanged a few words of small talk. Her accent was

3

North American but I was not able to pinpoint it to any particular country or region. She asked me not to take pictures, but said I could record our conversations as long as I promised to delete everything after it was transcribed. I showed her my portable digital recorder, and also a backup wireless pendant microphone which sent the audio directly to my phone. She was fine with both.

My visuals of her had been very accurate. She was around 4'11", small build, and very fine features with big eyes. Indeed very much like a porcelain doll. From her demeanor and clothes, I guessed she must be in her 50s. The feeling that I was looking into space, or into black transparent glass, was amplified tenfold.

There was also a distinct reserved air about her, like a cloud or mask that presents one person, while the true person remains invisible.

*** Have you read *Interview with an Alien?* ***

Yes I have. I like it! It's very relevant and timeless. It helped me realize why our friend came into my life when she did, but mostly I think she sent me the book so I could find out about you. Telling my story is not something that comes naturally for me. I am used to working in the shadows, in secrecy.

*** I would love to talk about your meeting with her, how she's doing and what you discussed. But I feel that this is not the story that wants to be told, am I right? ***

Right. It's not the story I am here to tell.

*** That's what I thought. OK, if you remember in that book our friend wanted me to present her interview as a novel. Would you like this book to be presented as a novel or as a real interview? ***

My thinking is that this information, along with what we are exploring over the next few days, is best presented as a novel. One reason is that it is not very objective, and secondly, the information is better received when the person reads it as thought it was fiction. Otherwise, the break in reality is too great. Or, something is triggered in the reader that makes them give up halfway through the book, missing important information.

*** Are there any signs our readers should watch for to know if they are being triggered or stopped before they finish the book? ***

Yes. There are several. If a person suddenly realizes that they can't remember the previous page, paragraph or entire chapter. Or, the feeling that there is too much information in a sentence or paragraph, like it's too dense. Another sign might be fear that what they are about to read is horrifying, polluting, or dangerous. At other times, the person could get dizzy or sleepy for no reason.

*** What should they do if that happens? ***

Read what you have just read a couple more times. If the symptoms persist, think to yourself "this is just a novel."

*** Thank you. That is very clear and simple. Do you think that what you have to share will transform people's lives? ***

Well, it will give them a better understanding of what is happening in the world today. At the very least, it offers a different perspective that will allow them to make more informed decisions.

*** When I look at you, you appear so... harmless and innocent. Yet there is a huge power I sense from you and my friend called you a "psychic assassin". Assassin means "murderer", which is a very strong word to describe anyone... I guess my question is, why the contradiction between what you do and how you look? ***

She smiled.

Interesting question to begin with. I thought you would ask me my age and place of birth. OK. Yes. I have killed people. It is not something I am proud of, or feel sorry about. I am not capable of having those feelings. Yet it is something that I recently realized was not correct. My physical appearance is like camouflage, it disarms people. In fact, most people don't even see me walk past them.

As she spoke these words, I sensed a very distinct feeling of self protection in her field. Self protection, but also protecting another or others. She became aware that I was observing that energy in her. She looked at me, her head angling to the side, her energy morphed into that of a rattle snake about to strike, then striking full force. I could even hear the rattle in my mind. It was fascinating. Her posture went back to a normal position and she looked into my eyes, frowning.

You are not afraid.

*** Hmmm… no. Do you think I should be? If so, why? What just happened? ***

You know, I don't think this is such a good idea after all. This interview. You can stay here and enjoy your time in Costa Rica. Thank you for coming all this way, and I apologise for wasting your time.

She stood up and held out her hand. In 2010, I had been asked to go public. It took me months to decide to do it, and since then there were aspects of myself that I no longer held back. I sensed similar energies in Ramona. I too had stepped into a role that was very different to the one I had in 2009 when I wrote the book, Interview with an Alien.

This was not going to be a regular interview, but more of an exploration. I took her hand, and allowed her to just Be. I've done this with hundred's of individuals around the world. It represents complete allowance to exist - without judgment... To be seen and connected in Oneness without expectations. It has always led to amazing shifts and transformations.

Her eyes opened wide, and filled with tears. She yanked her hand away and turned to leave. As she approached the door, she suddenly stopped, turned around, walked back and sat down again.

What the hell are you???

*** You might think of me as a blip in the program. A string of consciousness. A means to deliver the message of empowerment. Or, that I don't exist at all. Perhaps even as a mother and wife from Sacramento, California, USA... Take your pick. ***

We sat in silence for a few minutes. I could feel her scanning me, rescanning, and scanning again... Making a decision.

I sensed you in my field, in areas that no other human being can enter. I was going to kill you, but was unable to. It was like striking at empty space. Or missing the target before I could even shoot. This is really strange, since it's never happened before... At the same time, it felt like you could feel the "weapon" hit you, yet did nothing. The topper was that you didn't seem to care either way, as if it wasn't there. Tell me: why can't I kill or even affect you?

*** I'm thinking there was a lack of agreement. The time for me to leave my body is way into the future, not today. And even if it was today, it's not something I am afraid of. When we are afraid of something, in our minds, and in our body, it is us saying that it can happen. Therefore we are agreeing to whatever makes us afraid, or whatever we are afraid will happen. Is this normal for you? To try kill someone you don't know and have just met? ***

No. It was a knee jerk reaction. Which is also very unusual for me, as I have been trained to never act from fear or any emotion. As I look at it now, it feels more like a program, not an emotional reaction. Something was placed in my field to kill whomever had your vibration and ability, the ability to reach the parts of me that are closed. It makes sense if we think of it as a program to remove certain elements from the planet, which is what I did for several decades.

*** Like a failsafe to remove me or those like me from your life before we get acquainted. It makes sense. Have you had contact with others with my frequency of vibration and abilities before? ***

No, I can't say I have. However, I've pinpointed the program - the one that made me attack you, and will dissolve it before we meet again. This really annoys me. I've spent the past three years regaining ownership of myself and my power, and then this appears. I wonder what other programs there are that can be used against others without my consent. I am so angry right now.

*** I think the key is "without your consent". Most of us react and make decisions from unconscious programs. Even though they are not decisions or reactions that are deadly to ourselves or others most of the time, they are still decisions. I think it is no coincidence that I was the first person you have met with both this skill and vibration. You had already decided that your own power, and lethal skills would not be used without your consent. By meeting me first, you have made sure that you did not, in fact, kill someone through unconsciously acting out a malevolent program placed inside your field... Do you see the connection? The program was activated, but you did not kill me. ***

Yes. I see the connection. That is a very empowering perspective to see this from. I'm not quite sure what to do now. To tell you the truth, I'm embarrassed bywhat happened. We just met, and your non-judgment of what happened is a little confusing too. I honestly don't know what to say.

*** I'd say, let's do this interview and tell the world how a person can be in the position you just found yourself in through the machinations of others. Let's start with your handler, your teacher. Tell me about this person. ***

Alright, I agree... let's do this. His name was Elwin. He entered my life when I was six years old.

I lived with my family in a small village not far from here. We didn't have much, but we had each other, my family and I. The floors in our house were made of hardened clay mud, we had our own well, which was a luxury there, and no electricity.

Elwin arrived in a huge black car with two other people. They wore grey suits and were giants to us. Huge, pale white gringos. Elwin, a man and a woman. One of them spoke Spanish with a funny accent.

They told my parents that they represented a world religious organization that gave gifted children full scholarships to an elite boarding school in the USA, all the way through degree programs at University. Included with the scholarship was a massive monthly allowance of $50 dollars per month, paid directly to my family. They said that they were recruiting from all of Latin America, and had been contacted by my school, indicating my teacher had entered me into the scholarship competition.

My parents were overwhelmed and grateful. These important people wanted to give their daughter a huge opportunity in life, and the family a huge amount of money, lifting them out of poverty.

We, country folk, are a trusting people. And my parents came from a culture that was easily impressed, but this culture is also very protective of their children. It took those three people in their grey suits and big black car several months to convince my parents to let me go to the USA. In fact, my father insisted he be allowed to travel with me to visit the school before making the final decision.

That visit impressed my father greatly. The school was a palace to us. A huge mansion filled with dormitories, beautifully appointed classrooms, a sports hall, and a cafeteria which resembled a four star restaurant. It was like stepping into a luxurious movie set since we had never seen anything like it in real life. Elwin travelled with us to the USA and finished the job of convincing my father that this was the best thing for me. After seeing the boarding school, this was not difficult to do. Even I loved it. My father signed the required papers designating Elwin as my legal guardian.

*** Before we talk more about Elwin, could you tell me if this was a real school? I'm asking because it sounds like a place I was taken to when I lived in England as a kid, but the one I was taken to was not a real school. ***

Yes, it was a real school. Most of the kids were regular high society boarders. But there was an underground area that only a few kids were taken to every day. The adults called it the "research labs", but we called it "the Dungeon". The Dungeon was where the psychic training took place.

*** So all this happened when you were six years old. Did they give you a period of adjustment or did they take you straight into training? ***

My father stayed with me for a week, and the moment he was driven to the airport Elwin took me for my initial "interview" with a person we will call Lord R. It was not at the school, but in a nearby city. Lord R's office was in an old building which smelled of tobacco and furniture wax. I was still crying that my daddy was gone, and so Elwin carried me in his arms. He sat me down in front of a huge oak desk and we waited for Lord R to arrive.

I could sense the energy change in the room the moment Lord R walked in. He had two other men with him - younger men with hidden guns. Elwin stood up straight and I could feel that he wanted me to impress Lord R, as if to say, "here is my find", something Elwin desperately wanted validated by him.

Lord R sat on the other side of the desk while watching me carefully… you could almost say 'studying me'. He lit a cigar. I could feel that he was a powerful man, and that no one there was more powerful. After a short while he told me, with gestures as I didn't speak English at the time, to come over and sit on his lap.

I said "no" and crossed my arms and frowning. Elwin tried to convince me, but I refused. There was something about that man I didn't like. And then I sensed it… there were "energetic tendrils" penetrating my senses. I immediately recognised it as something I had felt when Elwin first arrived at our house. But with Elwin there was no "redness" to the feeling. No malice. I followed the redness back to Lord R, and I was able to see what it was. It was fear. It was as if he was trying to show me how powerful he was, and that he was an authority, but really he was afraid of me. It was very strange.

*** Did you ever find out why he was afraid of you? ***

It felt like someone accustomed to holding fire in their hands to burn others with, but there is nothing really to stop the fire from hurting them too, and they know that they can be burned if the fire realized there was nothing to stop it burning the person holding it. But I didn't understand why he was afraid of me for many years. At the time it just felt uncomfortable.

*** What happened after that? ***

10

Lord R stood up and made himself very big and scary. I started crying and ran to Elwin, which made the Lord feel powerful enough, so we were permitted to leave.

*** Sounds like a sick man. ***

Looking back I can tell you it was a good thing that he had taken a dislike to me, or was afraid of me. There were several cases of girls and boys being taken out of the school in the middle of the night, and when they got back they smelled of cigar, alcohol and furniture wax. Sexual abuse is rampant in those power circles, including abuse of their own children, the elite kids.

*** I've heard of it. David Icke talks quite a lot about it, and now there are witnesses coming forward that involved the Vatican, European monarchies and high level politicians. Did you experience sexual abuse as a kid? ***

I noticed her frowning, like trying to remember something.

I remember once I was dressed up in this beautiful white and pink dress. It had lace and ribbons and made me feel like a princess. I was told that I would be going to meet some important people and that I was very special. It was really late at night, but after that all I remember is a man telling me to go away. I was taken back to the school and the adults were very upset. It felt like I had done something wrong, or that I was not special enough. Of course, when I got older I realized that for whatever reason I was spared a nasty experience. But I do have large gaps in my memory. Maybe stuff that I chose to forget because it was too hard or painful for me to remember. So the answer to your question I guess is, "not that I know of."

At this point we decided to take a break. Sometimes, when we explore something, we need time to let a thought, memory or an aha moment to sit with us while we do other things.

The hotel surrounded its guests with luxury and beauty, so we decided to take a dip in the pool and enjoy the live band they had brought in for the day.

Chapter Two: Second Interview

Ramona and I met for breakfast, an amazing array of Costa Rica's cuisine and fresh fruits and vegetables. After breakfast we moved to the lounge and continued our interview.

*** Yesterday, you started telling us about your introduction to the Dungeon. Can you tell us what followed after your initial interview with Lord R? Was he part of the training program? ***

He was not actively involved in the experiments or training. But he did visit the school every six months or so. Everyone got very upset and nervous when he visited. As an adult I learned that all the staff were subjected to control through guilt. The person is seduced, or forced to commit an act so despicable that they can't really live with themselves unless they make it something "normal" in their minds. Since every other person in the place is also doing those things, it does become normal to them. Deep down they know it's not right, and that is the energy that is used to manipulate them, to make them work there without question. It is an abuse of power in the extreme. So, even though he was not part of the training, he was always present. When I was put in the field, he was the head of the agency I worked for, so I was interacting with him most weeks.

My training began the same day I met Lord R. If you could call it training. Elwin took me back to the Dungeon where they did all sorts of medical tests. The tests were regular medical tests, blood work, x-rays, lungs, heart, with just about everything examined.

I was then placed in a room with other kids and we were given lunch, or dinner. It was difficult to tell what time it was in the dungeon as there were no windows there. The other kids varied in age from around three to twelve years old. None of them spoke Spanish so I was not able to talk to them, but we had a lot of fun anyway. After that I was introduced to my school class and teacher. She was lovely... can't remember her name though.

The days became very blurred for the next few months. I would be taken out of class at all sorts of random times to do exercises which explored telepathy, telekinesis, and other skills. I would often wake

13

up the next day in my bed with no clear recollection of even going there. For the first year or so things were really cool and my English became fluent. I remember liking it there quite a lot and the crying finally stopped for my parents back in Costa Rica.

This is one of the things I find difficult about all this. The fact is that these people were very good to me. I received everything a little kid needs: love, attention, nurturing, education, thoughtful attention, and more. The staff became like my family, and the kids, the long term kids, were my brothers and sisters.

Apart from seeing the kids that had been abused, and discovering what the adults had done, there were no obvious indications during my life then or after, that there was anything wrong.

In fact, I was brought up to believe in the sanctity of the planet, how we have to protect the innocent, how we have to ensure that society is there to serve the people and that ...

She stopped talking. I could tell that we had touched on something that was a game changer for her. The thing that had made her "change sides".

... and that the elimination of six and a half billion people from the planet was for humanity's best interest.

*** Wait, I've heard of that before. There are some stones, the Georgia Guidestones[1], that talk about humanity being maintained at 500 million people on the planet. Were the people who trained you the same group that set up the stones? ***

---

[1] A granite monument standing in one of the highest hills of Elbert County, Georgia, the following is written in ten different languages: 1. Maintain humanity under 500,000,000 in perpetual balance with nature. 2. Guide reproduction wisely - improving fitness and diversity. 3. Unite humanity with a living new language. 4. Rule passion - faith - tradition - and all things with tempered reason. 5. Protect people and nations with fair laws and just courts. 6. Let all nations rule internally resolving external disputes in a world court. 7. Avoid petty laws and useless officials. 8. Balance personal rights with social duties. 9. Prize truth - beauty - love - seeking harmony with the infinite. 10. Be not a cancer on the earth - Leave room for nature - Leave room for nature.

14

I don't actually know. I am familiar with the stones and know that a lot of those sentiments were taught to me while I was growing up. You have to understand something else. The majority of the people whom you call the "Illuminati" or "powers that were", really, truly believe that they are doing all they do for the good of humanity and our planet.

*** I don't want to veer off from your personal story into a political discussion, but are you saying that things such as the multiple wars and false flag scenarios that the illuminati have carried out for the past decade, are being done for our own good? ***

Basically yes. If you think about it, and put it in your own words, nothing happens without consent. If we take that to an extreme, we could say that anyone who consents to be a victim of a malevolent government that throws them into a war, or affected by the poisons in chemtrails, or given vaccinations that kill their lineages, will be killed. It is not about the survival of the fittest, it is about the death of the weakest, nature's true working model. Not just the fittest survive in nature, but the average and not so weak do as well. Only the weakest get eliminated in nature.

If we translate that to what the Illuminati are doing now, from their own viewpoint, they are ensuring that the weakest are removed. And if you look at it a bit further, the strongest and the average are those who have woken up and are actively countering and disagreeing with what the Illuminati are doing. They are the ones who refuse vaccinations for themselves or their kids. The awakening ones are distilling or filtering their water before drinking it, refusing to eat corporate grown battery cage animals and GMO foods.

*** Well, I can see that point of view, but I have also known personally of individuals who have been murdered by these same groups, through cancer and other illnesses, or with bullets, who were breaking ground in areas such as free energy, technology and spiritual awareness that could rocket fuel us into the next paradigm. ***

I guess we are having a political discussion after all!

We burst out laughing.

15

There is a reason for that too. The "decision makers" feel that we, as a society, are not ready to embrace those technologies or awarenesses because we are carrying the weak people who are not willing to step into their own power. And that's why those groundbreaking individuals died, because they agreed that the time was not right yet. Plus they were weak too, in victim mode or fear mode. Anyone who thinks they can be hurt, will be hurt. It's like a Catch 22.

*** Well, I'll have to think about that one. Do you personally agree with those beliefs? ***

I did for many years. Most of my life in fact. But recently, I realized there was a flaw in the theory. The flaw is that if this was truly the case, then why are most of the people who are at the top of the food chain, the Illuminati, shadow government and the like, placed there through the abuse of kids and the inner guilt and terror that they not only perpetuate but carry with them all the time? Why are they their very own definition of what they would call a "weak" person that needs to be culled? Yet they somehow believe they are also at the top of the food chain?

When I started asking these questions, I realized that it is all a hall of mirrors, mirrors that hide something much larger, and that we can't really shrink everything to such simplified equations.

Things like free energy, for example, is just tapping into technology that is really basic, and many who are researching it are making it far more complicated than it needs to be.

*** How do you know this? What technology are you comparing it to? ***

I know you are familiar with how our shadow planetary government has been dealing with alien species, and harvesting alien technology. Well, the basis of alien technology is free energy. And by free, it means that it comes out from our infinite potential, not from a physical fuel or source. Not even from the Sun, or environment.

*** Oh my God. I have so many questions about this topic. A lot about the technology, but also about the government's alien contact. I guess we can start with free energy. You said it doesn't come from our environment. So, where does it come from? ***

OK, let's think about it this way. In every account that has been partly released to the public about alien contact, it has always been some sort of technology, a spaceship, and also living alien beings who were in the ship, right?

*** Yes, I've yet to hear of a spaceship that was remotely controlled. That didn't have pilots in it. ***

Yes. I have to think how to explain this in linear terms. In a way that makes sense.

So far we have technology and sentient beings, humanoids, inside the technology. And somehow they are able to travel through time and space quickly and efficiently, leaving no trace of radioactive, or any other type of fuel energy behind.

*** But I've heard of radioactivity being detected in people who have been abducted, or radioactivity left on the ground and trees around landing areas. ***

Those are most probably human crafts created from human attempts to reverse engineer alien technology. They tried to join conventional fuels with the alien technology... doesn't really work very efficiently. It's like trying to use a horse to power an airplane. With enough horses you can get the plane down the runway, but it can't really fly. Having people think that those human ships are alien ships also serves a purpose.

*** OK, let's not go down the road of humans pretending to be aliens, that's a whole book in itself probably! Let's go back to the free energy and how it's used. ***

Right. Have you ever had the experience that if you had a strong emotion - say anger or happiness, where light bulbs became brighter... Or even exploded? Or perhaps TVs, cell phones or radios stopped working, or computers burned up?

*** Yes, some of those things for sure. A couple of times the circuitry inside the object had melted. And also, I learned very early on not to touch electrical switches or outlets when I was feeling strong emotions because they would send out a painful electrical arc into my hand... and that hurt! ***

That's an example of your own energy field converted into electrical current, or heat, in the machine or circuit that's nearby. A human's energy field varies in strength, vibration and frequency depending on what they are doing, feeling and intending. But really, it's all still just energy, and energy can be tapped into and expressed in many ways. On our planet we are stuck thinking that the only way to generate energy in a useful form requires that we turn a mechanical, or kinetic device, to produce electrical energy. Even when we harvest energy from the Sun, we usually use it to heat something up, which then turns a generator that generates electricity. We are stuck in that mindframe, and any free power generators that are given the freedom to be developed work under this same model. Why? Because it is a model that's old and ensnares us in a cycle of energetic codependency. Like trying to power an airplane with horses. We still say that engines have *horsepower!*

What alien technology really uses, is the energy field of humanoids, which is directly harvested by the material the ship is made out of. The two become as one... a symbiotic relationship between the ship and the pilot or pilots. In this case, the mechanical, or kinetic function is the end result, not the a step to make a usable form of energy, such as electricity.

*** That raises the question of where that energy field comes from. Is it our physical body or emotional body? Could it be our soul? ***

Well, think about it this way: if you are feeling stressed or sad, your physical body will get very tired very soon. When you are feeling happy and inspired, you could physically go on forever. People who are in love often lose their appetite and don't even need food to keep them going.

*** So, the higher the vibration the person is in, the more powerful their energy field? ***

Kind of. It's more a case of energy flow, less physical resources are needed to generate it. Do you see the difference?

*** Not quite. ***

When we are angry, sad or upset, we generate a huge energy field, but a lot of the fuel for it comes from the physical body. That's why being angry, stressed or sad will usually make people physically tired. Ask anyone who has suffered from depression, they can hardly get out of bed. It's not just because they don't want to face the world, it's because they are physically exhausted. This can often cause them to overeat too. They are trying to fuel up.

When a person is very happy, in love, or inspired in any way, they have tons of energy. They can go on for hours without sleep, food, or even water sometimes.

*** Oh wow. This is linked to our consumption of food to keep us alive isn't' it? ***

Yes. There is a link between our emotions, vibrational level, and our physical bodies at the level of energy and power management. Survival through the ingestion of energy from the environment is very much linked together.

*** The implications of this information are huge. If we were to investigate this further it would change the way we think about food and all our current consumption of physical resources. ***

Yes. And think about this for a moment. Why do you think that so much money is spent to keep people at low vibrational levels in society?

*** Well, it's so that their awareness field is kept limited. So that their survival fear makes them willing slaves to other's will. So that they can play the victim/aggressor game and will not step into their power. So that they don't create a reality free from the shackles of enslavement. ***

Yes, and "stepping into their power" would also happen in a literal sense. They would literally have power to fuel their body and all of

19

their technological devices. The enslavement only works because people are stuck in the need to consume matter for energy and survival. It is literally a self feeding cycle. People believe they need food to physically survive, And this same model carries on with every technology they use - from their cars, to computers, books, even this very book being read - all these things 'need' material resources to exist. But what if the reverse were true? That a person's energy field could actually feed their physical body and the things in their environment?

*** Which it can. ***

That's right.

*** But the alien ships, their technology, that's made of raw materials too. I held a piece of metal in my hand and it was solid. It also was asking me for instructions. ***

Well, the use of materials to create objects, whether houses, clothes or spaceships, is not the same as using materials to create energy. That use of materials has a different purpose. I'm curious about the metal you touched. You say it was asking for instructions. That's something else that we haven't tapped into fully yet.

There haven't been any alien spaceships shot down by conventional weapons. What has happened in all the cases I've looked at, is that some types of our communication and detection technology can interfere with the communication between the pilots and their ship.

Most people, including the scientists that are busy reverse-engineering those ships, automatically believe that the ships carry the pilots. But in fact, it's the pilots that carry the ships.

*** Why would the pilots want to carry ships? It seems crazy. ***

Why do you carry a purse or backpack? Imagine you could travel the world in your house. That you could take your house with you wherever you went. Your house has lots of functions, but getting you there is not one of them.

*** This is radical. It completely changes the concepts we have about space travel and what we need to actually travel. How come those scientists and governments are not using this knowledge to develop spaceships that really work? ***

My guess is that someone wants to keep the model of consumption going. If they remove the need for resource consumption, the entire system collapses. They are also aware that we are a collective species, that what one person learns, will quickly spread throughout the collective. So training people to tap into their inner power, using their energy field to not just fuel themselves, but also a ship, is very dangerous for them. Anything that makes a person no longer dependent on their environment, fuel and resources for survival is controlled, ridiculed, or kept extremely secret. Still, there are plenty of stories from "insiders" who say these technologies have been developed successfully and have been in use secretly for decades. It's a very fine line that's been played using and developing this technology, while simultaneously ridiculing it publicly... since we are having this conversation, I'd suggest their model of consumption is collapsing anyway, just as they fear, and from their very own 'secret' use...

*** I can see that. I'm curious, how do you know all this stuff about aliens and their technology? ***

I met a few. The only way to communicate with most alien species that have had direct contact with us is through telepathy. But the real reason that I was allowed to meet them was not so that I could be a communication device for the shadow government. It was because they wanted to weaponize their technology. Instead of generating the fuel we might need for our needs, the agency wanted to find out how our own body's energy field could be used to kill targets reliably and on demand.

***Psychic assassins. ***

Yes.

*** I guess they succeeded. ***

Yes.

Chapter Three: Interview Three

The implications of what Ramona had shared were huge. There was a lot to think about. It didn't really surprise me that the government had decided to weaponize the knowledge about our energy field. But I needed to sit with the concept that stepping into our power had implications for our powergrid. I know, and have seen, that our emotional bodies are the key aspect that brings energy and causes the creation of physical reality, but had never thought of them as fuel.

We decided to take a break and meet again for lunch.

*** This morning you told me how the human energy field was weaponized. What I don't understand is why the shadow government is not afraid of that? Why would they let you and others learn how to use their energy field to kill people if this knowledge could spread into the human collective? ***

Making human weapons has been in the works for decades. For example, genetic engineering, hybrid programs, transhumanism, psychic and mind control programs, are all designed to create the ultimate human soldier. A "Super Soldier". Some of these programs have been successful. I was a successful soldier, and the reason the skill doesn't spread is because it works on the level of guilt, fear, and the destruction of other human beings. Our collective seems to be wired so that only knowledge that expands our capacity to survive and flourish spreads quickly and efficiently throughout the world in a few years, sometimes months. On the other hand, anything that lowers our survival chances has to be forced in.

Weaponizing one of our natural abilities has a twofold effect. One of them is that the shadow government has an effective weapon. The other effect is that the message the human collective receives is that this ability is deadly or dangerous, and people around the planet start putting barriers and blocks in front of the ability, making it more and more difficult for the masses to access. Another side effect, and one that the shadow government encourages, is that the collective becomes afraid to develop, or be around those with developed psychic abilities.

*** I'm wondering what we can do to counter that. ***

The fear of our own power is the biggest block most people have on the planet, followed closely by the fear of other people's power.

*** So what is needed is a massive fear processing[2] campaign focused on individuals fear of their own power. ***

That would do it.

*** Is this the main reason teleportation, biolocation and other skills are also blocked in our collective consciousness? ***

Yes. And the programming that blocks us can also be ingrained into the human collective by torturing and killing individuals who do have those skills. This is the main reason so many people were labeled witches and tortured horribly before being killed in slow and painful ways throughout our history. A reason they were burned alive. A past life experience of torture, abuse, and painful death because a person could use psychic tools would certainly censure the natural curiosity many are now experiencing in regards to these skills and abilities. Even... no, especially, if the memory of that previous lifetime is not remembered. The witnessing of the killing of others due to their skills and abilities, also ingrained an unconscious fear to have those skills. And in modern times it is carried out with the incarceration and drugging of millions of people who have displayed psychic skills around the planet by labeling them as having psychiatric conditions. I'm not saying that all people who need psychiatric help are psychic, some really are in need of medical help.

*** This data is going to revolutionize our planet. Once people become aware of why they are afraid of their own power, and what they can really do with it, nothing can stop us. ***

Pretty much. We haven't even started tapping into what we can do with our energy field in real life terms. The aliens we have had

---

[2] In my website ascension101.com, under the Tools menu, there is an excellent fear processing exercise. The full text is there available for free.

official contact with have capacities, yes, but I could tell they were limited, or they only revealed a small portion of what they can do.

*** Wow, that's exciting to consider... Let's get back to the topic of aliens. I'm wondering, did you ever meet any beings from other planets in real life? Or was your connection with them telepathic in nature? ***

I've met them in real life.

*** That's amazing! Which species? ***

I've met individuals of the species that is popularly known for their crash in Roswell in 1947, known as the Greys. I've also met a reptilian species, who seem to get way too much credit for running our shadow government if you ask me. But there are more... many more. I've only met the ones connected to my work, but I've heard there are about 72 known and documented species with a physical presence interacting on Earth at this time.

They all communicate telepathically, but the reptilians and the Anunnaki also control and subjugate other species, and their own populations, through the use of psychic abilities. The reptilians were of particular interest because they can trigger terror or any other emotion in a person's body whenever they want, and even make a person do things, like walk away, or kill someone, or even themselves for that matter. The ability to control others is something particular individuals of our human population can do, and it is something that I was trained to utilize very effectively.

*** So these alien species taught you how to do these things? ***

No. I was allowed to spend time with them as a member of a psychic communication team. But while I was communicating, I was also scanning them, and learning by watching how they did things. It wasn't difficult to learn and discover some of our own 'hidden' talents by seeing what they could do. If they can do it, we can do it. Simple...

*** Yes, I'm aware that we, as humans, learn the fastest by watching others do things. Map to others, as it were. Did you learn how to counteract their abilities to control and psychically 'see' you and scan you themselves? ***

Yes, there are two ways to counteract those abilities that I know of, one is to not react automatically to your body's terror and fear, and the other is to not blindly follow orders. It is crucial to learn how to not follow orders just because another person, or being, tells you they are superior to you. Realizing that the feeling, or belief, that the other being is way superior or is so strong, that we automatically do what they tell us, is false. Know that the belief that they are superior is just an illusion. It's not real. It's usually an agreement given out of fear, unconsciously. Automatically. Programmed and stimulated from archaic survival instincts. We are continually programmed to accept unquestioned orders from those we've been taught have authority over us.

*** So, processing one's fear, and not giving away one's power or authority are the major tool to retaining our own autonomy, sovereignty, and ability to function unhindered or be interfered with... ***

Exactly.

*** Well, I've been delivering that message to the masses for years now. ***

It doesn't surprise me. I can't figure out what you are yet, but I can tell that you have been on the right track. It would be very hard to stop you.

I sensed with her last few words there was a sting in her field, like a subroutine running in the background. I knew immediately that our meeting would be concluded in one of only two ways. Either I would successfully interview her and write this book, or one of Ramona's subroutines would find a mortal Achilles Heel of mine, and she would take me out. There was no middle ground here... I scanned her awareness field to see if she was conscious of this subroutine, but she was not. I was too curious to see how our week together would conclude, so I didn't bother to mention my sensing of her subroutine. Plus I was very interested in how her training was carried out, and what happened during her meetings with aliens to just walk away at this point.

*** How old were you when you met your first aliens, and what species were they? ***

I was ten years old. There were eight kids in my team, plus around thirty or so adults. We were shown films and given lots of information before we were allowed to see or interact with the aliens.

*** Were the kids and adults all from your school? ***

No, actually there was no one else there from my school. I was the only one. It doesn't surprise me though, most of the 'gifted' kids in my school were broken by the time they were my age.

*** What do you mean broken? ***

The training involved a lot of terror, fear, and physical pain. Also days of sensory deprivation in large tanks of thick liquid, where we were suspended with just a breathing apparatus protecting our faces. Often, children would have total breakdowns or sometimes suffer from constant amnesia. They wouldn't know who I was even though we'd lived together for years. Most were taken away and I never saw them again. I think some may have been reprogrammed or turned into sleepers. What I mean by 'sleepers' in this instance are people who can be activated to commit crimes or do other things triggered by key sounds, visuals, or other advanced technological methods.

*** Like the movies that show a person saying a key word over a phone and the sleeper goes and murders someone? ***

Like that, except as far as I know, it takes a sophisticated chain of words, sounds and visuals to activate them. Otherwise, if it was just a word, they would get triggered whenever another person said the word, which would be too risky. It does happen "accidentally" on occasion anyway, which does create problems for the handlers. Like a password for your computer account, the triggers have become more and more sophisticated as accidents became more frequent.

*** How many kids made it out of your school, and how many schools are you aware of? There must be quite a few if you didn't recognize anyone right? ***

Well, I made it of course, although I do have blank spaces in my memory. And there is also a girl and a boy that I know who made it out of that particular school. They are both alive, and still work for the shadow government. As to how many others schools there are? Well, I know there are more schools but I don't know where they are or how many there are. I can't imagine there are many. One would think that by now their methodology would be more sophisticated, so there would be less collateral damage. Less kids turned into vegetables.

*** Ok, back to what happened when you interacted with the aliens. Can you give us a step by step account? ***

The ones we call Greys were the first ones we interacted with. Even then, they weren't all purely 'Greys' since many of them looked like human/grey hybrids.

They placed me and the other kids in a room with books, toys, and snacks, and then they brought one of the Greys in. Holy cow, his telepathic ability was so strong. I stopped dead in my tracks, and so did another kid, a boy. The rest of the children took a few seconds to realize the alien was in the room. And I say the grey was a he, but actually there was no specific gender to it.

I became aware of his experience of being as he began tuning in to my experience of being... or my thoughts. It felt a little like the tuning of a radio, going back and forth until you get a clear sound, only it was not sound. I heard... felt experience. It was like sharing a story in feeling, videos, music, but not in words. Suddenly, one of the kids screamed and relieved himself in the room. The alien was taken away, and so were we.

The next time we met him, it was just me and the other boy who had immediately sensed the Grey in the room. They brought the alien in a wheelchair. He seemed really weak that second time. We played with toys, the three of us, the boy, the alien and I, shared about our homes and lives using that shared experience telepathic method, and generally had a really nice time. But after it was over, the people in charge took me to a separate room and questioned me for hours. It was horrible. Even though they were being nice to me, they kept asking me the same question over and over, plus I could feel the alien's distress somewhere in the building, it was really horrible. I thought at the time that they were torturing this alien, trying to get him to tell us about his technology and weapons.

It turned out that there were several Greys in the base. That they had come to stay, but they didn't live very long. Our atmosphere and foods were incompatible with their biology. The next time I met the alien, he told me he was just sick and that's why I could feel his distress. I asked him all the questions that the handlers wanted me to ask him, but knew the answers before he even shared them. They were here to make cultural contact and exchange, and they had even brought a few of their ships into the base to be reversed engineered. They did not carry weapons.

This went on for weeks. Eventually the other boy and I were allowed to spend time with other members of that species. The months I spent there, I think I must have met at least ten different alien Greys.

*** Do you know why these aliens chose to have cultural contact and exchange with military organizations rather than educational organizations, or even different cultures that might be more open to collaboration rather than exploitation? ***

Although I never confirmed it, the feeling I got was that they purposely chose the most violent and aggressive of our species to have a physical exchange with on purpose. What that purpose was, and whether it was malevolent or benevolent to us globally, I could never figure out.

*** Do you remember what year it was when you first met them? And where? ***

I couldn't tell you where, except that we flew in from the school, then travelled through some underground tunnels for hours. Looking at some data since then, I believe it was probably New Mexico. The year was 1968.

*** Are these the same species that abduct people to take genetic material from them? ***

Probably. That was not a question that ever came up. But their broad range of looks from completely different to us, to some who looked like human kids with large heads, I'd say there had been a lot of hybrid work being done by these beings using human DNA.

*** Did this contact end? Or did it go on indefinitely? ***

I was there and had daily contact with them for months. I can't tell how long exactly as apart from an hour per day when we were allowed to play outside, we spent the rest of our time underground.

*** Do you recall why the contact stopped? ***

One day I was told that I would be going back to the school, and that was that. I was not allowed to say goodbye or see the aliens or the boy again. By then I was well trained not to question my orders.

*** What did you learn from these Greys? ***

A very rich form of telepathy. Very effective. That's about it though.

*** Did you ever see them again? ***

I didn't see them again until I was involved in a car accident. At the moment of impact, I was pulled out of the car, and I found myself in one of their ships. At least I think it was a ship, but it could very well have been some sort of underground base.

*** They saved your life? ***

Yes. Apparently they had kept an eye on me my entire life, and for whatever reason, I guess I was not ready to die just yet, and they were there to intervene.

To tell you the truth, I actually drove the car off a cliff on purpose. At least I made sure there were no houses or roads at the bottom of the cliff, just rocks and the sea.

*** You mean you tried to kill yourself? ***

That's right. I'd had enough. And at the time it felt like I couldn't just walk away you know? They were holding my family and friends over me. It was made clear to me that if I didn't do as I was told my friends and family would be eliminated.

*** Yeah, I've been threatened with that too. ***

How did you stop them from carrying out their threats?

*** I didn't. I simply realized that every single friend and relative has a higher self, and that if they came to play a victim aggressor cycle there's actually nothing I can do to get them out of it except to disagree myself to play that cycle with them. And I was right. ***

Well, that would have saved me years of distress and heartache. It's so refreshing to hear.

*** What did you do to stop them? ***

I killed everyone in the agency who knew who my family and friends were.

*** I suppose from an assassins mindset, that works. ***

Not really, there's always new people who manage to dig deep enough to find out. It's a never ending battle. I'm not sure if I can do what you did, it's really hard not to protect them. And what if I'm wrong? What if their higher self wants them to have a victim aggressor experience, and they get tortured and killed? Wouldn't I be a part of it then? I guess I'll have to work on that.

Thanks for sharing another way to look at this. I see it can be very effective if I can get past the fear myself.

*** No problem. Tell me what happened when you found yourself with the Greys after the cliff incident. ***

I like that... my "cliff incident". Great way to describe it. I'm going to borrow that!

Ok, well, there I was, and there they were. I honestly can't tell you if I had met any of them in person before because their individual minds seem to mesh together with others. Like looking from a tree to a forest, to a tree again. That makes it very difficult to recognize each as an individual after some time, probably because they aren't a single individual mind.

In spite of my death wish at the time, I had a lot of questions for them, but I ended up being distracted by their desire to show me around. It was like they had been expecting me, and wanted to show me certain things, technology, people, the planet. Like a history of our planet - and more. After a few hours I found myself standing by the side of the road where I had driven my car off the cliff.

*** I get a lot of messages from people who have had abduction experiences with the Greys. Even in my family there are at least five individuals who are taken regularly. Some people say that the Greys are the most horrific, cruel and thoughtless creatures in the universe, that they do experiments, force pregnancies, steal sperm, ovum and fetuses. That they literally torture people. Others tell me that they have been looked after and nurtured by the Greys since they were babies, and that they have whole families in their ships, many being direct relatives. So, what gives? What are they really like, from your experience? ***

My experience with them has been positive. But I can see how some people would experience certain procedures as negative, especially if they become semi-conscious during them. I think that what's happening is that these beings are a species that relies on other species DNA for their genetic health. They harvest DNA and hybridize babies with us for their own survival and reproductive needs. I'm certain they do not abuse the resulting children, and do not torture people out of malice, although I think, yes, maybe sometimes out of ignorance. This stuff has been going on for hundreds of years really. But

32

recently, especially now, humans are becoming more and more conscious and are remembering things that in the past they have forgotten with the smallest amount of telepathic programming.

*** So do you think this race is benevolent toward humanity? ***

I didn't say that. But I don't think they are malevolent. In fact, I know they are not malevolent toward us. They are not on one side or the other, probably why we see them as grey. Not black or white.

People don't seem to realize that if the Greys were malevolent, considering their abilities and technology, they could have wiped us out completely a long time ago. No question about it. But they are not benevolent either. They just don't really have any intention toward us besides their own requirements, whether good or bad. They just live along with us and take what they need. Do they give back? Well, in my case they did, and I've heard of cases where people have been cured of terminal illnesses or received treatment for illnesses that human doctors could not treat. So, is it like a farmer looking after his cows? I really don't think so, but I didn't ask them either. When I was up, or down, or wherever I was there with them, I felt nothing but love and concern from them.

I definitely got a recharge of positive thinking and understanding from them. A 'cure' for my suicidal emotional exhaustion. And from that day on, I have not felt alone again. It's like something familial got reconnected.

*** Do you think you are related to them? Could they be your star family? ***

I know I'm not. It's not that. It's almost like they fixed something that was broken in my energy field. Something that connects me to the rest of humanity, to my family.

*** Ah, yes. I get it. ***

I noticed she had poured some sugar on the table and was drawing an infinity symbol with her finger on it. Over and over.

This symbol comforts me when something like a thought or a topic gets too big. It brings me back to my center. I recall that when I was with them that last time, I felt a sense that in several timelines, and outside linear time, perhaps where we might think of as our future, we created the greys. I saw that they were actually our children, our own creations. It feels like they are trying to find their way back to us. It's really difficult to understand a story like this that is so far outside our own reality and concept of time.

I was originally brought to them so I could learn how to communicate telepathically properly, but also to see if I could gather information about their weapons... no human there could imagine a species who did not carry weapons. Those people were certain the Greys must have weapons of mass destruction. I suppose if we think of them as our great-great-grandchildren, then yes, at some point, those Greys had weapons of mass destruction.

But I'm not sure if I understood correctly, that we created them as in we, human beings, created them, or whether we as the original creators for the universe, now playing at being limited humans, created them.

*** When you said that, it almost felt like they are an artificial intelligence. Like they don't really have souls like a human would. Like a very intelligent biological computer. Or perhaps souls that got stuck in computers. Like the Grey bodies are a biological ship, like a metal ship that travels through space. Something to carry an awareness, a soul that is actually housed in a body which exists in a different dimension or planet. I don't know. ***

Pinocchio trying to be a real boy.

We sat in silence.

Chapter Four: Interview Four

Ramona decided to spend the rest of the day and evening by herself. It gave me a chance to go to the beach and float in the sea for a while. I had a lot to think about and to digest too.

The next day we met for breakfast and Ramona said she wanted me to meet someone at a nearby village. I hadn't been out of the hotel resort, so was very happy for an opportunity to see more of Costa Rica.

We drove for about two hours inland, to a small village by the Guanacaste National Park. Ramona parked the car and we walked down a pedestrian street. Tiny houses lined each side of the road, their doors and windows open. The meticulously kept yards and decorative details were absolutely stunning. I was really amazed at the level of beauty and care even the most humble of houses had. The doors were carved, the dirt floors brushed. Not a spec of dust or garbage anywhere.

She noticed me admiring the beauty around me.

In many countries around the world poverty is the same as ugliness, garbage, graffiti, and human degeneration, the breakdown of human relationships, and a decline into violent crime. But poverty and those aspects of human reality are actually not related.

Anyway, here we are.

We stopped in front of one of the houses and Ramona shouted a greeting. Although hard to detect, I sensed a dissonance inside. Something that did not belong was inside the house. It felt cold and liquid. Like a leaky faucet in an old, damp, tiled bathroom. When I get visuals as cues, they are not to be understood literally. They are representations of what the images mean to me personally. And a leaky faucet in an old, damp, tiled bathroom, with the smells that go with it, meant there was something that was once well established, that dealt with cleansing, but was now abandoned and was leaking energy. The sound of the leaking drops bouncing off the cracked tiles could represent a clear energy residual echoing out.

An old lady came out and greeted Ramona warmly, then showed us in. She told us to go ahead into the back yard while she made us some fresh fruit juice.

The back was well shaded from the heat of the day, fruit trees and vines covered most of the small space. That's where he was sitting. A tall white male, probably in his 40s, blue t-shirt, jeans, sneakers, his legs covered in a blanket, his eyes slowly meeting ours.

This is Chad.

*** I see. Ramona, why did you bring me here? Who is Chad? ***

He was the last person I "killed" for them.

She stood there looking at me silently until the old lady came out carrying a tray with three colorful plastic glasses filled with freshly made fruit juice. After we took our glasses the old lady sat next to Chad, helping him drink his. Ramona and I sat down with them, and listened as the old lady told us of Chad's progress, which appeared to be nil.

It was a routine assignment. Chad was progressing into the creation of social communities based on human values and relationships that were not linked to labor or enslavement. When I was assigned to him, he was in the process of forming ideas. He was exploring ways to form a community where our capacity to create was truly and fully explored. Where technology, nature, and human beings were valued and used to support and nurture everyone.

He was just at the level of conceptual exploration. He hadn't even talked to or explored the ideas with many people, just a handful of his friends. No one had yet managed to even grasp at what he was reaching for. What he was developing in his mind.

New, dangerous ideas of community that are so outside of our present reality, that most of us can't even imagine them. Try yourself to conceive of a way of living together where no one has a role, or a job, as those things are not important or even exist.

*** If he hadn't even managed to bring forth a working model, or even put his ideas forth to many people, or anyone, then how did you know of it? How did your agency know of him? ***

We have technology, a method to join several individuals, through a bio mechanical computer, that creates a form of Artificially Intelligent monitoring system that can tap into the mind of every person alive. The machine is programmed to identify blips that can break the current system. Blips that can shift our society into a different timeline. Blips that change how we perceive ourselves and the way in which we accept what is real and what is not.

It works like a Geiger Counter that can detect different types of radiation. Once the blip is detected, it can quickly be located. Most blips are tiny. Maybe a conversation, someone reading a book that triggers a memory or an alternative timeline, or has a new thought. Those blips are easily erased by the machine. You would recognize them as suddenly not remembering what you just read, the past paragraph or page, or not remembering what you were thinking about or talking about. Sometimes a person forgets the topic completely and repeats the conversation all over again, only to forget it again. Sometimes it's like a feeling that you don't want to follow that thought anymore, or read what you are reading any more, or you stop watching something, or stop talking about something because you are afraid that it will never go away. Like it will pollute you. Or it's dangerous. So you stop.

If the machine can't remove the blip, one of us is sent in to deal with it.

*** Chad's thoughts were a blip. ***

Yes. His thoughts were a big blip.

*** Why didn't you kill him? ***

We were never supposed to meet. I'm never supposed to meet my target in real life. Normally, a person will be assigned to me, I will scan for them, and decide if I need to get closer to them geographically, or whether they have enough fear, or some sort of desire, so I can trigger the elimination of the blip from afar.

*** Wait, before we go on, can you tell me exactly how it is that you use to trigger their death? ***

Well, first of all, eliminating, or killing a blip doesn't usually mean killing the person. All we need to do is remove the blip, the radiation. Sometimes that means killing the person, but most of the time it means psychically killing the thoughts, or the continued pursuit of the blip.

Basically it is the removal of the energy, skills, or knowledge that could potentially veer all of us into a different society or culture as a species. Whether the person stays alive, or is killed is not that important.

*** So remove the radiation. OK. How do you do that? And how do you choose whom to physically kill and whom to allow to live? ***

No two people are the same. But, most people are afraid, or want or need something very badly. They have some sort of fear, want, agenda, or need. Once we identify what that something is, we activate or stimulate it. If the person continues with their pursuit of the blip, then we will go for their physical bodies. Sometimes they can be persuaded through threats, or seduced into their other desires, or their bodies caused to activate some sort of sickness that will either highly distract or kill them.

*** You can activate things like cancer? ***

Well, cancer is one of those illnesses that are often linked with emotions such as anger and fear. So yes.

There was a case where we were able to remove several individuals who were linked by a common interest by triggering cancer in just one of them and letting the rest know that we had caused this person's cancer. It spread like… cancer. But most of the time it's one person at a time.

But we don't trigger illnesses that often.
38

*** What other ways do you use to kill the person themselves? ***

We scan for physical weaknesses. A weak heart, lungs, veins in the brain, clots in the body, anything like that can be used. And then we use telekinesis, or an electrical jolt of energy from our own energy body to exploit the weakness.

*** What happens if a person doesn't have any exploitable weak points, whether physically or emotionally, or mentally? ***

When we can't reach a person because they simply don't have a fear, need, agenda or desire that's strong enough to manipulate, especially noticeable when they are first born or are still kids, we target the other children or adults around them. We basically use people who are asleep around them to make life hell for them. After that, we just feed the feeling of "I am sick and tired of this", with regard to life and their work, and also, "this is too much, too painful. I'm done." regarding life in general. We also feed the feeling of disconnect. Like the person is all alone in the world. Sometimes we even make a sleeper physically kill the person. If we have managed to get the person tired enough of life, they will die.

And the use of people who are asleep, that's something we learned from the alien reptilian species. Who are not that alien actually. And by people who are asleep, in this instance, I don't mean programmed by the shadow government. I mean people who you might call sheeple, or who have not chosen to become awake. People stuck in drama and low level human experience.

*** Yes, I've seen this at work. How those people can be manipulated remotely to do stuff. Before we talk about the alien reptilians, can you tell me what happened with Chad? ***

Ramona sighed very deeply and reached over taking Chad's hand in hers.

We were never supposed to meet.

He was assigned to me five years ago. The preliminary scans showed that he had no major items that could be exploited, they were not strong enough for me to detect fully or use at a distance.

He was in Brussels, so I flew to France.

He'd been in Brussels for two years and was living with a group of people in a house at an old historic neighborhood. It was a dysfunctional commune. A lot of pot smoking, vegetarianism, plenty of in-house drama, an alcoholic, and some seriously out of integrity actions. They shared a bitterness about society, the world and a lot of other energies that I could easily use in the group to attack Chad.

But he was untouchable. Even when I triggered a huge dramatic episode with the alcoholic, Chad breezed right through the house without touching the drama for weeks. It was like watching a ballet, a dance, where the chaos simply moves out of the way as the main dancer moves through.

Chad's an architect by trade, and unlike the majority of the commune members, he was gainfully employed. So the next step was to try to find targets at his workplace.

That one failed from the get go. I triggered other people with competition, jealousy, fear of job loss, fear of losing contracts, people using computers for illegal activities, causing viruses to break the entire system down, I tried everything and everyone I could find - even the office landlord and the janitor. Nothing would touch Chad.

When everything I had tried failed, I moved closer... to Mons in Belgium, about forty miles from Chad.

*** Can you explain why geographical distance affects your work? ***

One might think it's about the geographical distance. But in fact it's about the number of people between you and your target.

*** Do you mean the amount of people who live between you and the target? ***

Yes. Or work there.

*** But in my experience, when you connect with someone, it's like they are right next to you. It doesn't matter where they are in the planet or how many people are between you and them. ***

That's true, when you connect with another person, when you have a conscious connection with them, then distance, or the amount of people between you and them is irrelevant. But we don't connect with our target. What we do is eliminate the blip. And although this could seem to be very similar, and yes, I can scan and read a person on the other side of the planet at any time, when we spend time affecting a person, or people around them, it's like having several radios or DVDs playing at maximum volume nonstop for months.

*** So you get tired. Overwhelmed. ***

Yes. And less effective. When we are closer to another person geographically, we are able to move in and out of their field more easily. That's why people who fall in love, for example, often move in together. And why people still commute to their offices, and companies still have central offices to gather their workers in. We have the technology that allows us to remove the need for company offices and allow workers to telecommute. Yet telecommuting has not taken over our work model. The reason is that people who go to work at an office, or the same building, enter into a specific field with each other that is related to the work they do. The transition to work while at home is a hard one, and not that many people can make it because the people at home have other energies, which are not work related.

And it's the reason why certain cities and towns seem to support or specialize in trades and crafts. You will find University cities, for example, which have the most renowned and successful colleges and schools. Some cities are known for fine arts and artists will flock there. Others have music. Others food. The list goes on and on.

Where we are, and who else is there, affects our field, and our effectiveness to enter another person's field.

*** I think I understand what you are saying. Did moving closer to Chad have any effect? ***

Whenever I move to a different geographical location, I take time to acclimate. I spend time getting to know the local energies, finding a quiet location to work from, rent an apartment if necessary. A good exercise is to people watch. I go to cafes and sit there, pretending to read a book, or staring at a laptop and just observe people, their fields, their energies, that type of thing. By now I was on this case for a year and a half and was taking a break while I acclimated to Mons which was something I needed badly.

*** Wow a year and a half. I thought that your work was go in, take the person out, then leave. I suppose I was thinking of the traditional assassin, with the big gun. Very quickly in and out. ***

Well, even those types of assassins will spend weeks, or months sometimes planning the killing depending on how well guarded the target is.

*** I suppose. So spending over a year on a person is normal? ***

I've known of cases where the person is worked on for decades because nothing seems to stick for long.

*** Why not just send in a regular assassin with a gun? ***

That's only possible some of the time. I'm not sure why, but some people are not allowed to be killed like that. Allowed by whom? I don't know. Plus when we eliminate the blip with the person's own shadows, it often means that *that* particular stream of consciousness gets polluted. This pollution helps to keep the blip from appearing in someone else. Killing someone with bullets only draws attention to what they were doing, and more people tap into the blip's stream of consciousness.

*** Plus sometimes the person just doesn't agree with being shot by being afraid of it, or believing that it will kill them. ***

Lack of agreement. Right.

*** You said you were acclimating to the new city. ***

Yes. I'd been there for about three weeks and had decided to move into an apartment. It was a Tuesday morning. Springtime, so lots of potted flowers everywhere. It was sunny that day, but still pretty cold. I got my coffee, then walked outside to sit, but when I got outside I decided it was too cold, so turned around to get back in and smashed right into him. It was Chad!

*** How on earth did you not sense him there? What was he doing there anyway? ***

Both good questions that immediately crossed my mind. Our coats were covered in hot coffee, I fell backward with the shock and crashed into someone's chair, then their table which tipped over onto the floor. All the time I could see him going from shock, to anger, to concern, grabbing at the air trying to stop my fall. His laptop bag flew in the opposite direction. People around us were moving out of the way, screaming it was horrific. I hit my head so hard, and the energetic shock of meeting my target was so great, that I lost consciousness.

*** You lost consciousness. ***

Yes.

*** You mean you fainted. ***

OK, yes, I fainted. Oh my god. I fainted like some delicate flower. It was the most embarrassing moment of my life. It left me wide open.

*** Was it just the physical connection or was it a personal connection with Chad that caused the shock? ***

He entered my field, so it was personal. As I woke up, he was cradling me in his arms, on the floor, like some pathetic creature terrified he had killed someone. A woman was patting a wet napkin on my face, and someone said the ambulance was on the way.

*** Oh my God. Talk about manifesting a dramatic incident. ***

It was not me. I did not do that. I never meet my targets in real life. Never. And never touch them physically.

*** But *somehow* you allowed yourself to be in that situation. ***

Well, yes, the whole intent was to get geographically closer to Chad. There were no clients or friends of his in Mons, so no reason for him to ever go there. I was not meant to meet him.

*** What happened next? ***

More comical relief. I screamed and tried to get away, but was so dizzy and there was coffee and food all over the floor, so I just wriggled there like a jellyfish, like a hysterical female helpless on the ground.

The woman kept telling me to calm down, that I was ok, that everything was ok. And Chad was just looking at me like he'd killed me or something. His eyes were covered in tears.

It dawned on me that it was too late, that I could not get away from this and if I kept acting like a crazy woman, things would get much worse. So I played the damsel in distress. I calmed down and asked them all what happened, where was I, and stuff like that. I felt like the kid who was found with her hand in the cookie jar and didn't know why. I felt exposed, like the entire world knew why I was there, what I was doing.

And Chad stroked my face and kissed my forehead saying, "you are ok, you are ok, thank God you are ok."

I mean, who kisses a complete stranger on the forehead!

Ramona's eyes filled with tears and she started biting her lips trying not to cry.

*** You fell in love. ***

She nodded. I was dumbfounded.

She looked at me like a lost kid too scared to ask for help. The old lady gave her a tissue and patted her on the hand. "Pobrecita mi amor" she kept saying, "my poor little love."

I could see this particular scene was something that had happened a lot. Like a loop that can't be broken. Where everyone knew their role, their reactions, and the experienced same end result. Nothing would change. Only now there was a new element. I was there. Like my being there might change things somehow. But there was nothing I could do. Chad was a mess and Ramona was... disabled.

*** Have you ever thought that there are people who do the opposite work that you do? That you were, in fact, being played to distraction? That *your* blip was silenced? ***

My words made no impression on Ramona. It was like they were never heard. Too outside her reality to even perceive. This in itself confirmed my thought. Someone was doing to Ramona, what Ramona had tried to do to Chad. But who? And how close were they? Did they too have an agency? A biomechanical computer?

Mirrors within mirrors. Ramona's words bounced around my head making me wonder how far the mirrors went and why was I there, in the middle of all it all. I would have to play my role to see how the scene concluded.

*** So he kissed you. What happened after that? ***

Ramona wiped her tears and took a deep breath.

Nothing out of the ordinary. The ambulance came, they took me to hospital to check for concussion, Chad arrived at the hospital a few minutes after I did, and we chatted. Well, he chatted. I just stared at him. I had no idea I was in love. I was just staring at him wondering what to do. It was like landing in a foreign country with no clothes on!

Before I knew it, he was helping me into a cab and to my hotel, then buying me lunch.

He was all over my field, in my skin, in my mind, and I was swimming in his field like a mindless fish swimming in circles and blowing bubbles.

I realized that the damage was too great, he would have to be given to someone else. And I panicked at the thought. That's when I decided to hide him. I would make sure that the blip was gone and that no one would ever find him again. But it could wait. I could tell his thoughts of a better society were not present when he was with me. I could tell that I was a source of great distraction to him and it wasn't just concern about my welfare, or guilt that he had knocked me over. Which he hadn't actually, I fell because I was trying to get away. He liked me.

Distracting someone with love and sex is done a lot. There are people who are programmed to think there's a soulmate out there for them, that they need to meet, and every few days the system will activate the need to find their soulmate in order to be complete and happy. Bingo. Most of their days and nights are spent obsessing over their loneliness or wanting to find "the one".

Others are sent a person who can resemble a soulmate. It doesn't take much skill, and it is a role that's easily played by those broken kids and adults from the agency, the sleepers. They meet and seduce the target. At first, love and connection is used to keep the target distracted. When the honeymoon period ends, psychological and sometimes physical abuse is used to disable the target, keeping them occupied with so much low vibrational drama that no positive blips can even enter their minds, let alone be generated.

*** Is that what you planned to do with Chad? ***

No. Well, in a way, yes. I thought that I could buy time by making him think I was into him, and that he would fall in love and I could distract him for a long time that way. In doing so, I would have time to find a way to truly protect him.

I don't know what I was thinking. I didn't even know what being in love felt like, so I didn't realize that I was already in love with him. I thought I was thinking rationally.

46

I looked at Chad, the echo was getting louder. Something was changing. My presence was affecting the scene.

I know. You want me to tell you how I made him end up like this.

*** I think we should leave Ramona. ***

Yes. You are right. I can't think straight seeing him like this. Plus there's nothing you can do right? For a moment I thought that perhaps that's why our friend sent you to me. That you could help Chad. Help me help him.

The echo was getting louder. I got up and grabbed Ramona's arm.

*** Let's go. ***

As we were leaving, I looked back and thought I saw the tiniest flicker of light inside Chad's eyes. I looked away and focused on getting Ramona out of there.

Chapter Five: Interview Five

I had been pulled into halls of mirrors in the past when I was actively involved in mystical undertakings. But finding a hall of mirrors in physical life, involving people's daily routine, that was new to me. One thing I did learn, was that halls of mirrors are either used to trap people in a maze, or hide someone where it's very hard to find them. Mirrors within mirrors. Who were the good guys, who were the bad. Who was each of us really working with? Who was playing who? Was it a trap? Or was it a hiding place?

I had two nights left in Costa Rica. I had come here to interview a psychic assassin, to find out how a person could be made to become a psychic assassin. From what I could see, Ramona was highly skilled and was in many ways unique. I wanted to find out more about her training, the technology used, and the agency she had worked for.

But now there was Chad.

He was one of those items that one does not want to see. We think that if we look away fast enough, we can pretend they don't exist. But who, or what, did not want me to see him? Was it Chad himself? Was he the one that was distracting Ramona? Or was it Ramona's firewalls around Chad, those she placed there to hide him, that were creating my avoidance? Or was it a third party who wanted me to give up and go? Or even a third party who wanted me to look more closely?

The next day, Ramona called my room telling me she was waiting for me. I showered and hurried down to the breakfast room.

I want to apologise. It was not fair of me to take you to Chad or to expect you to heal him or something. I know you don't do that type of stuff.

I realized that I wanted to find out what was happening and that the information I had come to gather no longer seemed so interesting. I wondered if the distraction was the point of the Chad mystery. Mysteries can be sentient traps. Mysteries have been used as tools to ensnare us into distraction, and sometimes lead us into larger traps. But I was here, and the story wanted to be heard.

The distant echo of a dripping faucet was getting louder and louder. He was waking up.

*** Tell me how he got like that, Ramona. What happened to Chad? ***

My plan to seduce him into distraction worked brilliantly for about four months. I had leased an apartment next to a park, and he was there daily. He practically moved in with me. I'd never been so happy in my life. It felt like what I was doing was ok because I was not pretending to be in love with him, I really was in love with him.

*** Did you report back to the agency that you had changed tactics? ***

No. We don't do that. We don't report back unless we are finished with a job, or can't handle it.

*** OK. What happened after the four months? ***

He started thinking about the new communities again. And this time it was horrible, it was like our relationship had made his consciousness stream even bigger and brighter than ever. It was transmitting like crazy - it was huge!

I tried everything, I tried sex, drama, I even tried to get pregnant. But the more I did, the bigger his blip got. He started making charts, drawings of the mechanics behind the new social structures. He started contacting people around the world. It was like our love was fueling the blip. And then I sensed it - the presence of another psychic assassin.

They had sent reinforcements.

Ramona looked up at me, I heard the rattle snake for a second.

*** You killed the assassin? ***

Yes.

Killing another assassin is simpler than you'd think. Imagine a hunter is stalking a deer. He is so focused on the deer, so careful not to give his position away, not to scare it before he's ready to shoot, so intense in making sure he doesn't miss his shot, or hit the deer in the wrong place and just injure it, that their awareness becomes very narrow. It's all focused on the deer and the gun, and their own body. Sneaking up and cutting the assassins' own throat, as it were, is as easy as pie.

*** A sneak attack. ***

In a way, yes. There was absolutely no way that the assassin could know that I was coming.

*** He didn't sense you in his field? When you scanned him, he didn't detect you? ***

No, he did not. I'm not sure if you are aware of this, but when we scan someone we leave an identifying trace energy. Our vibrational signature. That signature contains information about our personality, our philosophical points of view, and even our genetic material. Like the program that activated when you scanned me, for example. It wasn't there to kill you personally, but anyone who had a particular vibration like the one that you carry within your signature.

*** What specifically can you tap into that is carried within an individual's signature? ***

From examining the actual vibration that triggered the program inside of me to kill you, I have concluded that it was a combination between the unrelentless intent to empower the masses combined with a particular genetic sequence.

*** Hmm, let me guess. You detected a certain genetic sequence related to a lineage that is carried by European ruling families. ***

Yes. You knew about it?

*** The fact that there are uncontrolled members of those lineages running around the planet is what scares certain factions of the ruling elite. It scares them that there are wild cards with a capacity to rule, as it were. So for them to create a firewall combining that particular genetic sequence and the empowerment of the masses vibration doesn't surprise me. ***

So you are aware that you are related to those monsters?

*** Absolutely. Although I wouldn't call them monsters, personally. ***

I don't know what to think. Sometimes I look at you and see the brightest light I have ever seen on anyone on the planet. But now as I look into your eyes, I see them. I see utter darkness. I see them in your eyes. I see those individuals as though they were looking through your eyes directly at me...

If I didn't trust our mutual friend so much, I would wonder what side you are on. What side you represent, support and empower.

*** Let's say I am on the side of global ascension and the empowerment of the masses. That, in itself, has no color, or side. It is just a game changer. But we are not here talk about me. Tell me how you managed to first of all scan, then track, then kill that assassin without being detected. ***

Now, you hold on just a minute. That brush off, the way you are trying to brush my question off is typical of their methodology, the way that those people work in the shadows. I want you to answer me straight. Are you, or are you not working for the ruling elites who are presently enslaving the human race?

I looked at Ramona. Sometimes when a person is deeply entrenched on one side of an argument, it's difficult for them to perceive that there is a whole world that exists outside of the argument.

*** I am not working for the ruling elite Ramona. ***

That does not sound like a complete response. If you are not working for the ruling elite, then who are you working for?

*** I'm not working for any side. To work for one side, means we empower the opposite side, and thus the duality of the equation gets more "real". When a person's awareness expands enough to be able to

52

make conscious choices, no one has power over what choices they make. The person can go in many directions, and that's the beauty of free will. I am not here to dictate or support the creation of a world ruled by light, or a world ruled by darkness. I am here to help expand each person's ability to make a conscious choice and not a choice made from programs, fears, or other beings agendas. What they do with that choice is up to them. They can go "light", they can go "dark" or they can go something completely different neither light or dark. ***

What if the person doesn't want to become conscious? What side are you on then?

*** For many years I worked on the assumption that every single human being wanted to become a fully conscious, empowered individual at a physical reality level. In 2011 the entire human collective's vibration and awareness reached a high enough level to allow each person to make a decision about how they wanted to experience physical reality. Each person had the capacity to make a choice, although in their daily life it might appear that they were still asleep, at a vibrational level they were conscious enough to decide how they wanted to live. The choice was between entering an empowered reality where a person knew they had full control of their physical experience, and a world where a person experienced a life where they were limited, disempowered and ruled by powerful humans somewhere else on the planet. A large percentage of the population chose to continue in an illusion of disempowerment. They were not done with it yet. This was a complete shock to me because of my personal assumptions that everyone would naturally choose to be more awake, aware, and self determined.

To answer your question, I have no sides. I was created by our own collective to ensure a fair game. A game where the choice of the collective, and each individual, is carried out in physical reality, which in itself is no more than a dream, an illusion. One could say that I am part of the dream, part of the dreamer, or part of the room where the dreamer is laying asleep. What they choose to do in their dream is not my concern, it should never have become my concern.

At a level of Oneness, even in a disempowered enslaved reality, the person is all parts including the jailed, the jailer and the jail... and the island where the jail is constructed. ***

I waited a few minutes, I knew this conversation had so many layers that it would soon be deleted from Ramona's mind and we could go back to finding out how a person can enter another person's field without being detected. And, just as I thought... she continued...

There was something I wanted to say, it felt important. But now I can't think of what it was. I'm sure it will come back to me. What were we talking about?

*** You were explaining about the assassin that came to deal with Chad's blip. You were about to tell me how you entered the assassin's field without being detected by him. ***

Well, it was because our vibration contained so many equal markers. When we are trained to do what we do, there are certain similarities. The training method followed, for example, is one that contains the capacity to do what we do, the skills, but also contains the "rightness" of what we do. Another common vibration is the assimilation of how we must follow orders, which includes the indoctrination of what our ethos, our belief system is.

To enter another beings field undetected, all I have to do is step through the vibrations that are the same as mine. Matching an assassin's vibrational field is naturally simple for me... even the intent to eliminate one's target is vibrationally identical. By making those vibrations strong, and making the rest very weak, one can be undetected in another person's field.

*** Did you physically kill the assassin? ***

Yes I did. He had a genetic disposition for strokes. He had a defective artery to the brain, a very thin wall which was about to pop at any time. I gave it a little push, the artery popped and the brain tissue began to fill with blood, causing too much pressure in the brain. He was dead within a few minutes. It was painless.

She looked at my neck, then my head.

*** That's how you tried to kill me too, huh! ***

I laughed. She smiled and nodded.

It's a wonder you are still alive, there are so many weak points in your physical body.

*** Yeah, I've died a few times already. But, the will of the collective to do this thing, to deliver this message, is stronger than my physical body's capacity to die. I can't really agree to that decision, dying, until my job is complete. Which brings me back to Chad. Did the assassin disable him before you managed to kill him? ***

No. He didn't get anywhere near Chad really. But once the assassin's signature was gone, gone from the planet, then all hell broke loose! I could sense them, the agency, trying to figure out what happened. I had been very careful, so they could not detect my actions. But they knew something was up, so I decided it was best to hide Chad. I put him in a coma. It was supposed to be temporary, with no long term damage done, but something went terribly wrong.

*** What happened? ***

Chad was in a coma so I had him hospitalized in a regular Belgian hospital. I went back to the Agency in the States. My plan was to turn in my resignation and then return to Belgium. I would bring Chad here, to Costa Rica, and bring him back out of his coma, then I would explain everything to him, and we would live happily ever after. Simple right?

Well, when I got back to the agency, Elwin was acting all weird. He was terrified of something. And he wasn't the only one. I told him that I was retiring, and he just said, "OK." and that was that. He went back to the school the next day and didn't even say goodbye.

I went to see Lord R, and when I gave him my resignation he just stood there laughing. He laughed and laughed... "You were always the odd one out Ramona," he said, "but I never realized it was because you were so stupid, so dense. You are probably the most pathetic, idiotic individual that has ever come through these doors. It's a wonder you made it to adulthood, and it's a mystery why you didn't break like the majority of these pathetic excuses for humanity we employ here."

Then he came for me, across the room, throwing chairs and everything in between us out of his way, he was in an absolute rage… I just stood there, petrified. He grabbed my face as I felt the other man in the room grab my arms. He stuffed my resignation letter into my mouth and just shouted and shouted obscenities at me, violently trying to make me eat the piece of paper.

*** Did you take them out like you did the assassin that came for Chad? ***

I can move and act very stealthily and effectively in the altered consciousness that we go into to do psychic work. But a physical assault is brutal, and my body went into terror. I remembered that terror growing up, the physical pain of torture, the panic that sets in after hours or days inside the sensory deprivation tanks. He knew exactly how to disarm me.

Suddenly though, something happened. I saw that redness in Lord R's energy field, the fear of the fire I had seen as a child the first time we met. It was like a lion tamer with his little whip, a whip he used since the lion was a cub. But the lion's teeth and claws could rip that whip and the trainer into shreds in a few seconds.

Lord R sensed my change, and I saw him nodding to the man holding me, I felt the man release my arm and start going for my head and neck. I could sense that he was going to break my neck. And that's when it kicked in. A skill I learned from the reptilians. The way in which they can make a body do their bidding. Suddenly, I 'became' the man who was about to break my neck. I took his gun with his own hand, and shot Lord R right in the head. He released me, and I turned around to look at him in the eyes. He was just a pawn. A soldier. He fell to his knees in a submissive position. "I pledge my service to you," he said, holding his gun out, handle toward me.

"Take me out of this place." I told him, and he did. People just moved out of the way as we walked through the corridors. He was Lord R's right hand man. Once we were out of the base, I told him he was free to do whatever he wanted. Oddly, he just stood there as I drove away.

The next few days were totally crazy. I went to the school, but Elwin said flatly that my family would be killed one by one if I didn't do as I was told. So I killed him, and destroyed all the records of me in the school, and the records of the other two people that knew of my family and where they lived.

*** The other two people who came for you with Elwin in Costa Rica. ***

That's right. But others have come, these past three years. Others have tried to reach me, have threatened my family.

*** I'm wondering Ramona, why you are willing to have your story published if the secrecy of your existence, Chad's existence and the existence of your family is of key importance to their survival. ***

Our mutual friend convinced me that the best place to hide is in plain sight. Besides, my plan isn't exactly working. Not only do they not stop coming for me, but Chad's brain damage is apparently irreversible. It's not exactly a "live happily ever after" situation.

*** Did someone, another assassin, get through to him after all? ***

That's the thing, I cannot detect any assassin's work. It was almost like something struck him when he was in the coma. Like something went in, and turned him into a vegetable. To this day, I don't know what, or who may have had a hand in it. I've scanned and rescanned. There is no vibrational signature. Nothing.

I wondered if she could detect the dripping water echo. If that echo had been there all the time, the past few years, it would have acted like a homing beacon for anyone searching for Chad. Yet I didn't detect it until we were right in front of that little house, and could only do so now because I was familiar with it. Somehow, Ramona was not able to detect it or she would have mentioned it. If her explanation of how we detect vibrations was right, it meant that that echo was made of a signature that was an integral part of Ramona's own signature. What could that be?

As I observed it, the echo, I felt Chad's consciousness come online. I looked at Ramona, but didn't detect any change in her demeanor. Ramona had probably given the old lady a cellphone to use any time she detected a change in Chad's health. In my estimation, it would take just a few minutes for the phone to ring.

I had a strong feeling as to how and why Chad was in the state he was in, but it was not something that would be well received by Ramona. I had to tread carefully.

*** Ramona, do you remember what you said to me about the first time Chad kissed you? After you physically met him? ***

That I was in shock? That he went to the hospital with me?

*** The actual words, after he kissed you on the forehead. ***

OK... hmm. I said, "who kisses a complete stranger on the forehead."

*** And do you remember what he was saying as you were coming to? ***

He was saying, "thank God you are OK."

*** And he was cradling you in his arms. ***

Yes. What's the point of all this? Why are you going over the details like that?

*** It's about your choice of words. Tell me who kisses a complete stranger on the forehead while cradling her in his arms." ***

No one does. But that's Chad, he's like that, so kind, loving, giving. If he thought he killed an innocent bystander, that's exactly how he would react.

*** He would kiss a stranger he thought he killed. ***

58

What are you getting at? I don't understand.

*** Looking from the outside in, Ramona, it feels to me that not only did Chad know you, but he was in fact already in love with you when you met. ***

But that's impossible. He didn't know I existed before that moment.

The phone was about to ring.

*** Before you answer the phone Ramona, please understand that it is not personal. Chad is as much of a pawn as you are. ***

What phone? What the hell are you talking about? You have to be more specific, clearer.

The phone rang.

I held her eyes for as long as possible. Delaying the phone conversation she was about to have, giving her enough pause to integrate the questions I had asked before she was told of Chad's miraculous return.

There were two possible ways in which she could react right now. One was to drop everything and run back to Chad, the second was for her to be open enough to see that there was more to Chad than a blip about community living.

She picked up the phone and had a short conversation in Spanish. She hung up and sat there, looking at me. Then started drinking her tea.

Who kisses a complete stranger on the forehead.

She said. Then answered her own question.

No one kisses a complete stranger on the forehead.

Inelia, I can grasp what you are implying. That Chad knew me. That he knew exactly who I was and what I was doing there. That he moved in for the kill when I was looking elsewhere, when I stopped looking at him and was getting familiar with Mons instead. You are saying he is a psychic assassin working for the other side right?

*** It's a possible conclusion to the evidence. Not the only conclusion, but a very probable one. What you need to determine is if perhaps someone was trying to disable both of you, or whether the real target was you, or was it indeed Chad all along, or the agency itself. After all, you did take out some key players at the agency. Players no outsider would have had access to.

To see what the point of it all was, step away from being a victim, or hunter, and see what resulted from all this. What happened. What is still happening even now. ***

I need to go. I have to see him. He's calling my name but he's not fully conscious yet. I'm sorry about this, but this interview is over. I have to take care of this situation.

*** I'll come with you. ***

She was about to say, "no, stay here," but she nodded instead. On our way out she insisted that the interview was over, but that I could record the events as long as I stayed out of her way and didn't interfere. I was curious to see her entire energy field changing, focusing, becoming sharp, like a knife, or bullet.

Chapter Six: Finding Chad

The following chapters will be written as a narration rather than an interview. Ramona basically refused to be "distracted with questions" from the moment we left the hotel to see Chad. What followed was an experience that broke many reality parameters for me, as well as for Ramona.

Beginning of narration:

By the time we got to the car, Ramona's phone rang again, apparently Chad managed to get away from the old lady and was nowhere to be found.

Ramona parked the car and tried to calm down enough to scan for him. We were in the middle of nowhere, fields around us, the damp heat of the day beating down on us.

The thought of the observer affecting the observed occurred to me as a possible explanation to Chad's recovery, but it was not likely. The leaky faucet type energy I had observed was there before I arrived in Costa Rica. That's why it felt like an old place, an old leak.

Ramona started banging her hands on the steering wheel, "I can't find him! I can't… stay calm."

But I could feel him. I could sense him at the edge of my awareness. Yet, if I entered his field it would change whatever path these two people were on. Becoming part of the story was not my idea of a good interview. However, these books are anything but passive explorations. When I interviewed my friend to explore Hybrid Aliens on Earth, not just our own lives had dramatically changed as a direct result of our exploration of the topics in the book, but thousands of other people's lives had been changed too as they read the book. Now, as I explored the training and skills of a psychic assassin, it wasn't just about exposing our shadow governments mechanizations for world domination. There was plenty of information about all that out there. This had something to do with the people involved, including me as the writer, Ramona and Chad as the channels, and the reader as the observer. *The observer affects the observed.*

I didn't want to find Chad, but I knew I had to.

I stepped out of the car, closed the door behind me and leaned against it. After a short while Ramona came out of the car and stood next to me.

"It's seriously hot and humid out here." I said.

Ramona put on her sunglasses on and said, "well... If I can't find him, I doubt anyone else at the agency will find him either. Please help me. Tell me where he is."

"To tell you the truth, I don't really want to." I responded.

"Why not? What's going on with you?"

"I'm not sure. It feels like a split in timelines. If I follow this line, to find Chad, I will open a door into a timeline that I cannot close behind me. And it's not just you, me and Chad who will be walking through it, but hundreds of thousands, maybe even millions of individuals who step into the journey by reading this book, maybe even these very words."

"But... if it is a bad timeline, then you can simply shelf the book. Delete it. You have deleted other books before, other timelines, right?" She asked.

"Yes. There was a book that I never finished or published. That door, I was able to close. I'm not sure if this one can be closed. It will affect everything."

She paused for a moment. "Ah. Our story, our journey, it itself is a blip that can be picked up by others. Something that acts like a virus in our human collective. If that's the case, then it's definitely worth pursuing. Only those blips that promote human evolution and welfare actually go viral. Everything else has to be pushed in with huge effort and force."

I smiled, "well, there has certainly not been any effort on my part to interviewing you. Tell me why did you chose Costa Rica for your base Ramona? I can tell that it's not because you were born here, or have family here. If anything, that would have made this location the last place for you to settle if you wanted to keep your relatives safe."

"The reason is the same as the reason why there is no army here. There are certain agreements, diplomatic and otherwise, that ensures a level of sovereignty here that no other country in the world has. It is also ..."

" ... it also what?" I asked.

"It's nothing. Nothing that affects us personally. It has to do with having a place on Earth that has a vibrational signature that does not contain the fear of invasion, or defence. Not just a geographical area, but a population of people who have not subscribed to the need of an army."

I felt into the energy when she talked about it. "It feels like an anchor across time/space. Like an energetic anchor from the future into the past, which we are experiencing as our present time. Hmm, an anchor that is outside time/space altogether. Outside the victim/aggressor insanity. Outside the reaches of the shadow government. A level of sanity that is clearly before its time."

"Well, not sure about that last one, the United Nations is a tool of the shadow government and there's United Nations University for Peace here." She said.

I have to admit that this bit of information took me by surprise. I'd never heard of a University for Peace before.

"Oh really? The UN has a satellite organization here? And it's related to peace? It would be fascinating to see what the university is like, what the people are like. What they are investigating and studying, that type of thing. An anchor here could be an attempt to learn something, or it can be a way to try to either vamparise or pollute the energy that exists here."

I closed my eyes. "I'm not sure why or how this relates to us finding Chad.

I don't know yet. But I do know it's related. For some reason, when I sense Chad, I feel the anchor outside of timespace. Listen - if we explore it, and people read about it, it will become a conscious factor at a collective level. We could go back to the hotel and continue talking about your personal experience, your training and the jobs you have carried out. Or we could pursue the connection between Chad and this anchor in time. If we do the second, then each individual reading about it will be an active participant in the lifting of the veil regarding something that is game changing for our species. "

"Can that happen? That people who read something in the future have an effect on it unfolding in the past? Wouldn't that mean that what is written is not solid even if it was written in the past?"

"Well, I've had situations where I read a book twice, and the second time around it's like I am reading a completely different book. More important, in this situation, I sense the readers are affecting how our experience turns out... They are influencing whether we make it out alive and the whole book gets published, or we die and only half the book gets seen. This is essentially affecting the depth of information that gets through, in other words... what we are able to uncover and talk about. Whether we go back to the hotel and talk about your personal experience, or see where Chad is leading us. Everything."

"Are you recording this? I have a feeling that we might forget this conversation in a few minutes."

"Absolutely. I have the recorder on."

I pointed to the pendant microphone which I had attached to my blouse that day, "yes, mic is on. And my phone is in my back pocket, receiving the audio."

[Note] As I transcribe the content of the recording, I have become aware that about two thirds of our discussion was gone from my memory.

I closed my eyes, it helped sometimes, when there was too much psychic noise to figure something out. I heard it from all around, it felt like it was coming from the future, and the environment around us. "The energy I am getting very powerfully, as I look into this, the fact that we are here, that Chad is awake, and our relationship to Costa Rica, is that we need to duck."

"What are you talking about? Duck?"

"Yes, basically to get out of the way. I think that bullets, energetic, or otherwise, are about to fly, and we need to get out of their way. And if we do get hit, it's not personal. It's not because of who we are, but where we are.

My connection to Chad suddenly became solid. "I guess we are stepping into the interesting timeline after all. We go after Chad. I can see him clearly now."

I pointed south east. We got back into the car, and Ramona drove while I gave her directions.

Chad's energy was as white as snow, and bright as the sun. Like clear white glass, looking into the brightest of snow covered landscapes on a brilliant sunny day. It was obvious he loved Ramona with all his heart. Then I picked up another energy.

"Ramona, Chad is not alone."

She listened into the energy, "yes, I can sense someone. More than one person. They don't feel threatening. They are in our field, but I still don't see Chad. Is he with them?"

"Yes. Or at least, he is on his way to meet them, or someone is taking him to them."

She nodded. "I can clearly hear their neutrality. They want to know that I will stay neutral, not attack. I'm not sure I can answer that."

"I think it's the intent they want to hear. Are you coming in with the intent to harm, or are you coming in with no intent to harm." I said.

Ramona responded, "my intent is to find Chad and take him home. If they get in my way, I will take the necessary steps to complete my mission."

I half expected the engine in the car to fail when she said that. But it didn't. I assumed that whomever had Chad did not have any intention of getting in Ramona's way.

We drove for several hours, and day turned into evening. I had to force Ramona to stop for food and a bathroom break at a small town. There was a bar and a handful of small stores on the main street.

We sat down at one of the tables in what was obviously a family run eatery. A few minutes later a man came with two plates of chicken soup, bread and utensils, followed by a bowl of salad and a plate of rice and beans. The fact that we were not asked what we wanted to eat, or that there was no menu, really surprised me. Ramona explained that these eateries were quite common in Costa Rica, and catered to the local workers. You eat what had been cooked that day.

I turned to Ramona and asked, "can you still sense the people who have Chad?"

"Yes, quite clearly. They feel … grey. Not as in the alien species… although they might be alien. But more in color. They also feel old. Very old. Or new. Not born yet. Advanced."

"It's the timelessness. The outside of linear time aspect of them." I added.

"Ah, yes. That explains it. Do you think that us talking about this, and giving our geographical area away will create or attract an influx of awakened individuals to Costa Rica?"

I wasn't sure. "It's possible. But at the end of the day, I think that people end up, or visit, where they are supposed to. And information comes their way for them to assess from all sorts of different directions, whether they act on it or not, really, is a very personal decision."

"Can you sense that there is no longer an urgency to us finding Chad now?" She asked.

"Gosh you are right. Yes, I can sense it."

She closed her eyes and became very quiet. Then smiled. "This is interesting. The urgency to find Chad is gone, and that can happen because we found him, or because he's safe, or because we are no longer being stopped. Or, and this would require enormous skill, we are being slowed down by making us feel there is no urgency in finding him."

"Do you know how to find out which it is? What reason is it that we no longer carry an energy of urgency?"

"Yes. What I am doing right now, is to sit with each possible reason. Allowing it to vibrate through my physical body and seeing if it creates any dissonance. The only one that is completely resonant for me is that we found him. He is here, in this town, or very close by."

We finished our meal, freshened up and walked out to wait by the car. I wasn't sure what we were waiting for, but somehow, we both knew we needed to wait.

The black sedan arrived about half an hour later. Tinted windows, very "men in black" in appearance. It completely clashed with the town, people and the environment we were in. It was way too shiny to begin with. Our own car was covered in dust from the day's drive, but the sedan was eerily clean. It stopped in front of our car but no one stepped out.

"I think we are meant to get in it." I said.

"Yes. Normally, that's not exactly a good idea... Let's do it anyway."

We laughed. It was crazy. We walked to the car and Ramona opened the back door, and climbed in. I opened the front passenger door and climbed in. The driver looked at us, nodded and we drove away.

"Hey, why didn't I think to ride shotgun!"

"You probably come from royalty, used to being driven around instead of sitting with the hired hand."

We laughed some more.

I tried to engage the driver in conversation, and he politely answered all my questions, except where we were heading. He addressed his employers as "los señores", which doesn't have a precise translation into English, but could be roughly translated, in this context, as "lords".

We drove slowly on small dirt roads for about twenty minutes. The town left way behind, no light except the car headlights. Around us only trees, no fields. We came to a very tall welded wire gate cutting across the road. The gate looked abandoned and unkempt, but opened automatically as we approached.

"He's here." Ramona stated.

I could sense Chad very close. "Yes, he is."

A few minutes later the trees parted giving way to a well lit rectangular structure. There were a handful of people visible either walking around or inside the building. We pulled up to what looked like the front door, and our driver wished us a good evening. We took the hint, got out of the car, and walked into the building.

"This way." Ramona turned to one of the corridors and started running. I followed closely behind.

She burst into a room. Inside was Chad who was not quite fully conscious and was insisting that he had to leave, while a young man appeared to be trying to calm him down. As soon as Chad saw Ramona he stumbled toward her and embraced her like he hadn't seen her for years. His speech was highly impaired, but his words could be made out, "you are alive, my love, you are alive. Don't leave me. Don't ever leave me again."

Ramona held him, and dissolved into his field. I could see she was crying silently, confused, and unable to act in any way but that of a being who is deeply in love and has recovered her lover from the claws of death.

The young man managed to convince Ramona to help Chad into a chair, where he then started taking Chad's blood pressure and temperature.

The energy field around Chad was very different now. It was still dissonant, but the energy that felt like a leaky faucet in an old bathroom, the drips echoing around the cracked walls, was now more like concentric lights expanding outward, bright, loud.

I sat next to Chad and took his hand in mine. He turned to look at me, the light in his eyes was flickering in and out. His body was shaking ever so slightly, like that tremor often found in people suffering from post traumatic stress.

The young man suddenly stopped working on Chad and faced the door, lowering his eyes to the ground. Both Ramona and I looked toward the door.

The door opened and an older man entered. His energy was neutral, and he was smiling.

"Welcome, both of you", he said.

Ramona's energy suddenly quietened. She sat up, and looked at me. I could tell she was out of her field of knowledge. This man's energy was not light or dark. Not an enemy or a friend, the two sides of reality she was familiar with. I couldn't make head or tail of him either, but knew that any reaction on my part could dictate what happened next. We were clearly outnumbered, and possibly energetically outgunned, so stepping into fear, or battle, was not an option.

I smiled back, and asked, "who do we have the pleasure of speaking with?"

"Call me Alaster."

"Nice to meet you Alaster," I said walking toward him and extending my hand in friendship. "I would introduce myself and my friend, but I suspect you know exactly who we are."

"I know what you both represent" he smiled, taking my hand, "you are the gate openers. The ones who bring the world's eyes with you."

"You appear to be the one opening the gate Alaster. We simply walked through it to reach Chad." I responded, walking back to Chad and Ramona.

"It's one of those situations where each of our parts were decided well before any of us were born, and also, at the same time, decided today when... neutrality was breached." He said.

I could tell he had struggled to find the right word to describe what exactly was breached. He had used the word "neutrality", but the word felt inadequate for what he meant. What he meant, I felt, was a state that transcended both light and dark. A state where neither existed.

"I..." he paused looking at me with curiosity, "don't know what you are."

"Join the club." Ramona said, half jokingly.

As it often happens when someone next to me is trying to figure out what and who I am, I am able to tap into their full energy signature. I scanned him, but could not find any point of familiarity to explain what I was perceiving. He was totally alien to me.

"You are not in the equation." He stated. It took me a few seconds to realize I had not seen his lips move, and that his clearly audible voice had sounded directly in my auditory perception and translation area of the brain. In other words, I heard his voice in my head.

"Whoa! How did you do that?"

"Do what?" Asked Ramona.

"Umm, he totally spoke into my brain. Not like telepathy, this was audible words using his voice."

Ramona looked at Alaster, "what did you say to her?"

Alaster looked from Ramona to me, then back to Ramona, I could tell he was not expecting that reaction from either of us.

"I… said… that she is not part of the equation."

"What equation?" Both Ramona and I asked.

"The one that's here. You, Ramona are what we might call a low vibrational soldier. Violence, war, conflict, the taking of lives, abuse of power, fear, terror, darkness. Chad is the opposite, he is peace, positive collaboration, nurturing energy, use of power, happiness, light. I am the absence of both of those opposite vibrational stands. But you," he said looking at me, "you are none of these. You are not in the equation. Yet, here you are, standing with us in this room."

I was not sure if that was a question, but I didn't have an answer if it was. What was I doing there anyway? Apart from following curiosity and wanting to know how Ramona's story progressed, I had no interest in what Alaster was, or what his people where doing here. But I should have been interested. I focused back on scanning Alaster. He became visually wobbly. Like something looked at through rippling water.

"You look like a regular man Alaster, yet the people here call you Lords. And you can project auditory information directly into my brain. This is not something I have seen other humans do without technological help. I suspect that your physical appearance is also a projection, and not the actual way you look?" I asked.

"Yes, you are correct in your assumption. Our physical appearance is humanoid, but not familiar to the human species, which makes it hard to have any sort of interaction with them when we are in our natural form."

I wanted to see what he really looked like, but knew my body would freak out. So held back in requesting him to show his true form.

The response came into my head directly again, "you are wise to choose not to see my true form. It would only be a source of distraction and not in any way beneficial."

I thought, "so you can hear my actual thoughts,"

"Yes, it is just a more subtle form of sound waves. Humans are very good now at thinking actual words. And not so good at keeping them to themselves. You are in a human body, and behave like a human."

I looked at Ramona, who was looking at me intently, she asked, "do I want to know what you guys are talking about in your minds?"

"I'm just curious about his auditory projection ability." I said, "I like to know how things work, and why." I turned back to Alaster, "back to this equation, the one that has you, Ramona and Chad in it. What does it mean? Why does it exist? What's the result supposed to be?"

He laughed. I could sense this might take some time, and that he was looking for a way to make it simple and easy to understand. A bit like one would try to find ways to communicate to a new born baby.

"The planet, well, your society, is entering a stage in its experience that requires peace and war to consolidate, as it were. You see, peace cannot exist in war, and war cannot exist in peace. Both are the absence of the other. That is what they are. That is why there are some areas of the planet that are in a state of war, and others that are in a state of peace. All relative to the other.

I am a member of a species that does not exist in war or peace, we have no concept, or reality, of either of these energies."

"When you say species, do you mean aliens?"

"No. We have populated Earth for a very long time. We have seen your species being born, grow and evolve into different forms and dimensions. We use this particular geographical location as a meeting place of different realities within our planet. Like a no man's land."

"Your planet?"

"Our, yours and ours... well, not sure about you personally, but humans and ours and many other species as well."

I was curious to find out what he knew about Earth, about Gaia, and how that compared to what I knew about her/him. But didn't want to change the subject from what was important here, which was this equation thing and how it had come to exist.

I had a sudden thought, and it was mine, I checked, "Ramona and Chad were never meant to be together right? They were both sent to eliminate the other, make the other non-existent, but what happened was that they joined in an energetic field and did not exterminate the other. Energetically, this seems impossible to do, for both fields, dark and light, to exist in the same space, but they did it."

Alaster moved closer to us, his body became more wobbly to me, I was finding it hard now to keep his illusory projection of a human body and could perceive his actual body coming through into my senses, but could not figure out what it was. The situation was indeed very distracting. I checked my body and noticed she was feeling some fear, I processed it and she agreed to stay calm. Thinking back to when we shook hands, he had felt rather cold and smooth to the touch. Reptilian perhaps? No, not quite.

He noticed my body's discomfort, realized and acknowledged that his visual projection was failing on me, and moved toward the other side of the bed, where Ramona was sitting. He was uncomfortable with his inability to keep the visual projection solid for me. I felt a type of apologetic energy, and an energy of surprise at his own failing to keep me comfortable.

I didn't really know how to respond to that.

"Yes," he nodded, "Ramona and Chad caused a glitch, a field, a vibration, like a ping, that resonated around the planet. But then it vanished for a few years. The vibration began again a few months back, and has been getting stronger ever since. We initially identified the origin and saw it was human in nature. We captured the mind of the most open of the two we had focused on, and guided him here. We knew the other human would follow quickly behind."

"I don't understand, why do you need them here? Why bring them here?"

"It's an opportunity. The field lasted only a few months the previous time and it was faint. Then it vanished. When we detected the field yet again, and that it was coming from humans who were so close to us physically, we knew that we had to bring them here. Otherwise they would certainly die. One or both of them would die."

I looked back at Ramona and Chad, wondering why it was so important to keep them alive, and how were they so unique on the planet that this strange species had brought them here. What was the nature of that field, and why had it manifested now, and with them?

"As long as they exist in the field they created," Alaster began explaining, "the human species is able to absorb and learn about this new field. A field were both dark and light exist as one. Not co-exist, not non-exist, but actually, literally, exist as a different vibration which is neither dark nor light, but both at the same time. A consolidation of sorts. Which is what we have been sensing as an alternative timeline for many people of Earth. Not just humans."

"Isn't that impossible? Doesn't that go against all the laws and rules of our reality?" Ramona asked.

"Well, yes. And that you would find your way here, so close to our place, is also impossible. But here you are. And we don't know why or how you made your way here."

The thought of another yet unidentified third party choreographing all this, moving people, including Ramona, Chad and Alaster's species, for their own ends entered our minds all at once. Alaster and Ramona looked at me, I could sense fear in their eyes.

I put my hands up in the universal sign of non-threat, "hey! don't look at me, I... am one of those pawn things too in this case. I'm just here to let people know this is happening. My readers and I have nothing to do with it - we are simple witnesses. Blame HER if you have to blame someone," I said pointing down at the ground.

Alaster and Ramona both looked at the ground, then at each other, and then back at me.

"Gaia! Blame Gaia, or blame the human collective, heck I don't know. I just have a habit of being in the… can't say right place at the right time, it's more like at the key place at the key time. Why? I don't know. But it happens. A lot. And for the record, I don't really have any judgment or care what you do with your reality, planet or anything else. All I am here to do is to make sure you all have a *conscious* choice when faced with the different timelines that are open to you."

"All of us?" Alaster said.

I realized that yes, it included his species too. I nodded.

Ramona nodded, and relaxed.

Alaster's shape suddenly shifted for a split second, becoming large and bright, definitely humanoid, then back to human. My body gasped. He blushed and apologised. Like someone would if they suddenly farted in polite company.

"Don't mention it." I said.

"Don't mention what? And what are you embarrassed about?" Ramona asked Alaster, as she could tell our exchange was not about their shared suspicion of me being the brains behind our present predicament.

"I am afraid that keeping an uninterrupted human form projection on your friend's mind is much harder than expected. It is taking a lot of my focus. And that makes it difficult to stay present in figuring out our current circumstances and how we should proceed."

I suddenly felt very uncomfortable in the room, in the entire building, and land they had here. I wanted to leave. I scanned my energy field to identify the origin of that uncomfortable feeling, and saw that it was a projection from whomever was observing the conversation, via some sort of visual and auditory technology that resembled our camera and television systems. But in this case, it was a full multi-dimensional experience, like a holographic movie that includes subtle energies, thoughts and emotions. All our mental chatter, energy body, emotional body, physical body, inner and outer conversations were being monitored, recorded and experienced by others.

I wanted to follow that energy line, that awareness field, the field that belonged to Alaster's species, but I KNEW I had to stay focused on Ramona and Chad. This was a key timeline split for our species. This was information that had to be perceived by thousands, if not millions, of people, including every single reader. Information that presented a different choice, one of not stepping back into the old paradigm, not stepping into the empowered, lighter paradigm, but stepping into a *completely different paradigm* where light and dark exist as one, where they don't exist as the absence of the other, and they don't "not exist", but exist as a completely new vibration. Not gray, which is the mixing of black and white, but a color that does not exist in our current spectrum.

Two psychic assassins, one working for the light, one working for the dark, sent to eliminate each other, falling in love, somehow joining their fields without knowing it, they both continued their work to eliminate the other, somehow staying at their respective end of the spectrum, yet with their physical closeness, within their energy bodies, something else began to emerge. Something unknown to this reality.

I found I had been making funny whistling sounds with my mouth while thinking, like a mixture of white noise and an old phone data connection as it sounded in the 80s when our computers dialed the internet. Ramona was looking at me curiously, while Alaster was covering his ears.

As I stopped, my mouth open to apologise to Alaster who was obviously distressed, but before I could say anything, several 'men' burst into the room, grabbing us, except Chad, who was now out cold on the bed. As I was dragged out of the room I saw Ramona being injected with something that knocked her unconscious. My thought was loud and clear, "Crap!" A cold smooth hand covered my mouth. Something about my whistling had turned on panic stations. "I"m sorry?" I thought as loud as I could, telling them whatever it was, was not intentional. But the pin prick on my arm was sharp and fast, I fell into a pit of nothingness. I recognized that pit, it was singular non-existence.

Chapter Seven: Fear You Are Welcome Here

When I woke up I was so relieved to be alive. Not particularly because I am attached to life, but because this was such a fascinating situation that I did not want to leave it without finding out more!

My body felt nauseous, and I started gagging before I could open my eyes. Someone sat me up and helped me as my body puked her last dinner out into a bucket.

I felt Alaster enter the room. His "human-ness" was diminished, and he was more purely his own self. As he really is, he doesn't have very many familiar energies for me to identify as emotions, feelings or other such human-like things. I opened my eyes and was relieved to see that he was still human in shape. Or at least my brain was still receiving his projection.

"What the hell Alaster," I managed to either voice or think. "Not cool." I added.

The person helping me, who I noticed was a regular human doctor, pulled my hair back from my face, helped lay me back down and fiddled with the intravenous drip stuck in my arm. She looked at Alaster, frowning at him, then back at me with a concerned, friendly face. "It was supposed to be a mild sedative. Your body is allergic to it and went into full anaphylactic shock. I am administering an adrenaline-based medication. I am also treating you with a native plant medicine that will help you recover back to full strength very quickly."

Alaster came closer to me, but I could sense he was restrained in some fashion. My brain felt muddled and wobbly. Bits of his projected voice, mixed with his wobbly body and the other people, his people, being part of the experience. One message came through loud and clear, "not human", and another vibration, the closest translation of that vibration to our reality would be "fear".

I put my mentally generated hand up, because my physical ones were non-responsive, and said, "excuse me, but I am as much human as you are... well, whatever species you are. This is one big misunderstanding, and I'd like to go home now. In fact, no. I demand to see Ramona and Chad. They are under my protection, so keep your cold hands off them."

I became aware that I sounded like a drunk person. Whatever sedative they had given me was still in my system, and I was as high as a kite. Still, making demands was a shot in the dark, but you never know what will work in situations like this. Right?

Alaster said something or other, then the only other human in the room, the doctor, left. I noticed four more wobbly bodies around me. Armed bodies!

"Oh, OK." I said, realizing that whatever that sound was that I had whistled, it had somehow breached their security. They could not keep me asleep, because my body reacted allergically to their normally harmless medication, and they had convinced themselves that I was not human. There was more going on, but I had not managed to figure out what it was just yet. My brain was still in a drugged fog.

"Ramona and Chad?" I asked.

"They are perfectly safe. We mean no harm, we simply need to proceed slowly with this. We are following all acceptable protocols here, and have broken no rules. We apologise for your unexpected death, have treated you back into life, and there is no long term damage to your body. In fact, we fixed a few things that were not functioning properly as well."

I found myself frowning. His words, and the way he delivered them, was almost like he was talking into a microphone. Then I figured it out. He was part of a species that had a conscious collective mind. Where one of them can be like a remote camera, a fully multi dimensional camera, to their entire collective. The human collective is in fact like that too, but presently not at a conscious level.

His species is conscious of their personal, and their collective consciousness. They are able to move in and out of one or the other at will.

He was not talking to me, he was talking to my "collective". He didn't believe I was human, he didn't know what I was, and I had somehow managed to breach their security, so for him, and his people, this was "first contact".

It took me a few seconds to realize that in fact I was like a microphone, a camera, to a very powerful collective. The human collective. Indeed, these events were being experienced by my collective, through the book, through reading these thoughts and words - once I put them down on paper, throughout time and space. With others around the world, you, the person reading these words, are watching, perceiving, seeing what I saw, felt, and experienced.

But he was not talking to the human collective. At least he didn't think so.

"Wait. You killed me?"

Alaster's body teetered in and out of his true form for a split second, and his human form blushed, again.

"It was not an act of aggression. We did not act in malice toward you. It was an accidental death, which is now fully reversed, as you can see, since you are alive and well now."

"What the hell Alaster, you killed me man. Not OK. And now you bring guns?" I said, looking at his companions.

"We are simply being... cautious."

I was finding the entire situation quite comical, and realized that it was probably the drugs, but perhaps it was just me and my wacky sense of humour. I could see their predicament. Question was, did I play along and use their obvious fear of me and my imaginary "collective" to get Ramona and Chad back on whatever course they were on? Or did I play it honest and admit that I had no idea what the hell was going on? I realized that I was thinking all that aloud (oops), and went quiet again.

I said, "cover your ears," and played the sound I had been whistling, but this time in my mind. Their reactions confirmed that it had the same effect, the other people in the room covered their ears, then stopped and pointed their weapons at me. This time the weapons were "switched on".

I smiled.

Alaster laughed.

"There is no overlay of data on that noise, it is just … noisy," he said, and waved the soldiers away. "I would like to know how you knew to do that. How you knew how to block us out."

"I didn't. It just happened. A lot of times I do stuff without having previously learned it myself. It just downloads directly from the human collective I suppose." I tried to sit up and he came over to help me, fixing the pillows on my back so I could stay sitting upright.

He didn't see me as a threat anymore, which was good. I've never felt comfortable with armed people around, so their leaving was a good thing as far as I was concerned. I wondered though, if he was from a species that did not know war or peace, why the guns?

"For someone who is not war or peace, you sure have a lot of weapons." I said.

"When dealing with humans, we have found that arms are necessary. We don't use them in malice, to conquer, or to gain power over others. In fact, we have never used them. It's more of a show, a communication device that humans and their governments understand."

"What exactly do those weapons do?"

"They transmit a wave of physical paralyzation and unconsciousness. It wipes the person's short term memories out too."

Before I could ask, he added, "no, you have not been shot with them."

"Alaster," I said, "we have a problem. Well, two problems. One is that whatever you are, has been kept secret by human governments, but with the publication of my book, everyone will begin to know about you. The second problem is that the energy field that Ramona and Chad created, well, that's not active if they are unconscious. How can it continue to be absorbed and shared within the human collective if they remain unconscious? Ramona is very dangerous and once you wake her up, and she sees what you did to her, she's going to react before she thinks or can be communicated with."

"We acted without malice…"

"Yes, I know," I interrupted, "but Ramona won't see it that way. Do you know what a psychic assassin is capable of?"

"Yes, we… read her life."

I knew that the word "read" was also short of describing what he meant. What he meant really was "living" her life in one moment. Where one is the other person, and experiences every moment of their life, in a few minutes.

Before I could enquire more, he said, "we need to understand how this new reality field was created by Ramona and Chad. We have read both of them, and don't see how it is possible. Other humans of opposing vibrations have physically joined together for life before, and they have not generated a new energetic field. What is so unique about these two individuals? We need to know."

I felt a clarity enter my awareness, and while I recognized it as a familiar voice, I could not identify it. It felt like Gaia, like a beautiful, motherly goddess of nature. Apparently, she was in stealth mode, and looked like a memory of a flower. I looked closer at Alaster, I was still very weak and groggy, but my mind appeared to be clearing up quickly. He was not aware of anyone else in the room. The energy in my field was so pristine, so clear, and I allowed myself to map to that clarity. "It's important," she said, "that you make it out alive. That you publish what you have seen. Leave this place now."

"What about Ramona and Chad?" I asked the flower.

"Leave them."

I continued looking at Alaster, he had not registered the consciousness that had entered my awareness. How was that even possible? I was exhausted, and could hardly breathe, let alone move, but I had been around the block a few times. It didn't take me very long to realize that the reason why Alaster had not registered a new consciousness in my awareness field was because there *was* no new consciousness in my awareness field.

It was *his* collective speaking to me directly. My first impression that it was someone like Gaia in stealth mode meant that the image and vibration they had projected was one that was highly resonant to me, but not necessarily a true essence or vibration. They had simply tuned their communication to a frequency that I would be expected to listen to and possibly obey. But I've never been good at taking orders, not even when given something believed by many to be Gods or Goddesses. If they had "read" me too, they would have known that.

I wasn't about to leave Ramona and Chad behind. They would have known that too. Obviously they could not 'read' me very well.

He frowned as he looked at me, it was clear I had not reacted the way they had expected. He relaxed and asked, "ok, what do you suggest then? How should we handle Ramona and Chad?"

This had to be thought out quite carefully, but I was still groggy and somewhat zoned out with the drug and the after effects of the allergic reaction.

"Yes," he said, "I apologize. You need to sleep so you can recover more quickly."

"That might be best." I said, and he nodded and left the room, closing the door behind him.

I turned to one side with great difficulty, as my body was still very unresponsive, and closed my eyes. The pillow smelled like all good hospital pillows, overly disinfected, boiled and steam pressed.

Whatever plant medicine the doctor had included in the intravenous drip was running through my veins and activating many senses. There was no way I was going to be able to sleep. Not with the plant and adrenaline in the mix. Although I was not really sure if there was still adrenaline in the drip or whether it was just the plant. Still, there was lots of adrenaline in my body and I was not going to sleep any time soon.

So I breathed in very deeply instead, relaxed my body and scanned outward, making my field larger and larger. I could sense the world outside the base, many underground levels, a labyrinth of tunnels and enormous cave-like structures, cities, in what felt like was "underground". I could not figure out if it was really underground in a physical sense or it was ultradimensionally placed. But it was using a space below what we commonly know of as the Earth's surface.

As I entered one of these cities, I felt the lights dim on an automatic switch of sorts that restricted visual information the moment I walked in. I could smell food, cooking of some kind. Flowers. Water, the energy of pure crystalline water. And what I interpreted to be the laughter of children.

The lights went dimmer and I could no longer sense the smells or hear the children. I scanned away and took one of the tunnels. It was long, and at some points it came close to the surface. It appears that these people do live in our physical world. Between our "crust", below the rocky area, and above the center. In fact, I could see several layers of habitable spaces underground, comprised of different ages, and different vibrations. Each were occupied by different species, subtleties, and energies. Some were abandoned long ago, and some are occupied, almost squatted in, by other beings. I was surprised at the size of our planet, at how many layers there were that were occupied, or had been occupied at some point. Had been occupied, abandoned, then re-found by another group even. Amazing.

The Lemurians, for example, were very close to the surface, but not quite.

I could not comprehend how there could be so many layers to the Earth. It just didn't add up. It felt physically impossible, but these layers were truly physical, not subtle or in other dimensions.

Alaster's people, the ones I did not have a name for yet, were very physical, and from a layer that was quite deep. But they did not share many points of familiarity with our own species. In their world there really was no light/dark paradigm. These particular polarities simply did not exist. It was almost like seeing the world through a color blind person's eyes, where certain colors simply could not be seen.

I could now also better understand this geographical area, and this base in particular. Alaster had called it a no-man's-land. But it was more than that. It was like a meeting point of different existences. And my original feeling that it was an anchor point between past, present and future, with regard lack of war and peace, was also right. This place seemed to exist outside linear time. Only it didn't. It reminded me of that trick one can do with a pen. You have a solid pen, hold it in the middle with the tips of your thumb and index finger, and move your hand up and down while quickly shaking the pen so it looks like the wings of a humming bird. Soon the solidly straight pen starts looking like it's soft and wobbly. Our perception says it's soft and wobbly, but stop moving it, and it becomes a solid straight pen again.

As my awareness came back to the surface of the planet, around the base, I noticed something like a cloud of heat. And it was trying to break through. Trying to get into the base. I touched it very briefly and recognized the energy immediately. It was Ramona's old agency. Their intent was to acquire the target and bring it back to the USA. So Alaster and his people were not the only ones to have detected the new field generated by Ramona and Chad. The agency had too, and it didn't take much imagination to figure out that Chad's organization was probably also out there trying to get in.

Her agency wanted to hijack the new element to tap into its power, or weaponize it. It made sense, they hijack a lot of energies, people, intents and situations. Power over others at its best.

I felt a solidity surrounding my body, it was a familiar, yet still unrecognized vibration. The best way to describe it is to think of it as an armor coming online moments before going into battle. This made no sense because I no longer do battle. I watched the solidity vibration closely, and saw that it had the signature of a "guardian". An impenetrable force that stands between something or someone and whatever is trying to get to it, him or her. The guardian armor has no judgment, fear, or aggression attached to it. It is simply an armor.

As I felt the armor becoming increasingly solid, I knew what had to be done with Ramona so that she wouldn't kill everyone around her the moment she came to. It was so simple. All I had to do was to surround her in the armor long enough for her to become aware of her actions, letting any rogue programs shoot, and simply let her use up her ammunition. After that, it would not take her long to take stock of the situation we were in and choose a better course of action. She was a highly intelligent woman.

I opened my eyes and was shocked to find the room was full of people. Well, full of Alaster's people. There were at least twenty individuals standing there, around the bed. Their human appearance wobbling in and out of focus. I looked quickly around for Alaster's familiar face, and found him near the wall to my left. Their attire was very different to anything I had ever seen before. They were wearing robes that looked like tunics, or cloaks, made of... well, lights and crystals. It was really beautiful to behold. I so wanted one of those robes.

"Can I have one of those robes?" The thought and words popped out of my mouth before I was able to register them. I closed my mouth quickly with some embarrassment. For me, this was like first contact with a group of what looked like ambassadors of an entire species, and my first words were to ask them for one of their robes.

They started looking at each other smiling. Alaster was nodding away in the back. What the hell was going on?

"We like you." It was a woman, a female, that spoke. She was also standing to my left, but right next to the bed.

"Thank you. I like you too."

What else could I say? Besides, I did like them. They were very pretty and their vibration was different and interesting.

"We are under attack." This time it was a man who spoke, he was near the door in front of me.

"Yes." I said, "I felt them, it's Ramona's agency. They want Ramona and Chad, so they can hijack the new… element."

They all looked at each other for a few moments, then back at me and the man spoke again, "we predicted that this would happen, which is why we brought the new element here. Ordinarily the agency would not be able to enter here because of their particular polarized vibration. We opened a door, so to speak, to let Ramona and Chad in, and although we closed it behind them, we cannot keep it closed for too long, and we cannot keep them in the base for too long, because this place, this area, will neutralize them."

I wondered what they meant by *neutralize them.*

"They will cease. Stop. End."

"Die?"

"We are not sure. This has never happened before." This was a man who looked decidedly older than the rest and was standing to my right. The others parted and he came over toward me. He reached for my hand and held it in his. His hand was warm, and his body was not wobbling in and out of his human shape.

"Wow," I said, "you are either very good at the mental projection thing, or you are human."

"I am human." He said. "My name is Sandro Renato."

"Italian?"

"About three thousand years ago I was born in that geographical area."

"About three thousand years ago? Wow."

He smiled,"well, you seem pretty human to me. Although I don't have the same depth of perception as my adopted nation does.

Perhaps one day we can sit down and compare notes. But at this very moment, we need to secure Ramona and Chad. You said you knew what to do with them?"

"Well, I know what to do with Ramona now. But I don't actually know what we can do with Ramona and Chad once they are awake. Why don't you take them to one of the underground cities? You are human and have obviously lived down there for a long time."

"Ramona and Chad have survived here this long because this is a no-man's-land. If we were to take them back to one of our cities, they would… cease to exist."

When Sandro said those words, I finally understood what they meant when they expressed a person would no longer exist. I said, "like vanish from the spectrum because their colors don't exist down there."

"Yes, something like that."

I nodded. It made sense. Everything we think exists is actually no more than perceptions interpreted by our physical bodies, including our minds. That's why we can only see a fraction of what is really going on around us. Our spectrum of perception is intentionally very small.

Everyone in the room looked at each other, nodding, then back at me, smiling.

I had to ask, "why are all of you looking at me?"

Everyone laughed but me.

A woman to my left responded, "we find you curious. We wanted to experience you first hand. Our species is separated into sub collective consciousnesses. Each person in this room represents one of those sub collectives. By having one of us in direct contact with you, the experience of your existence is felt more clearly than if we use a person who is part of a different collective. We are all, of course, part of the whole, but each subgroup exists in a slightly different resonance. And within each collective, each individual is able to come in and out of their own personal consciousness, their larger subgroup consciousness and the entire collective consciousness."

"Oh, just like humans." I said, "only you do it consciously."

"Yes," that was the woman again. "May I touch you?"

"Sure," I said. My entire life I had been asked, "what are you?" And there was no complete answer I could give. In their own way, this species were asking the same thing, but the answer was unimportant and irrelevant at this point. What I found worked best in situations where the question came up, not that I had ever had a situation exactly like this this one before, was to explain myself as it related to whatever was happening at the time.

Even though the question of what I was had not been asked directly by them, I decided to answer it anyway, I wanted things to get moving.

"Well, most of my life I have been a wild card. I've simply fitted where something was missing or I was needed to make something else complete. At the moment, I am the armor you need to bring Ramona back into full consciousness. And then, if you are able, I would suggest you fix Chad's brain damage so he too can be fully functional. We are going to need them both for what's coming next."

They all looked at each other again, this time it seemed like for several minutes, then nodded and left the room. Before Alaster left, he said, "I will send the doctor in to help you get up and dressed."

Chapter Eight: Containment

It wasn't going to be easy to get Ramona back to full consciousness without her going all Rambo on everyone present.

I sat with her, and found they had her in the same room as Chad, in fact on the same bed. Our hosts might not be human but they sure did understand people. Even though both Chad and Ramona were sedated, their bodies would be able to feel the other's energy field and proximity, making them much more relaxed and less stressed. It was beautiful to see actually. Their hands were literally touching, her pinky wrapped around his thumb.

The room was so grey, the bed so neutral, metal, white sheets, a familiar clinical smell about the place. It felt like it needed flowers, a coat of paint on the walls, perhaps lilac? Green? Yellow? or a mural, like a deep forest.

Suddenly I got it. I could take them into a lucid dream, or an astral construct of a forest, or other beautiful location, and have the initial conscious conversation there. Maybe Gaia might lend a hand and provide an actual physical location to land in. I knew that a construct like that would not contain Ramona for long, but it would give her enough confused time to connect with her, and tell her what was happening.

Just thinking about the deep forest provided an intimate link with Gaia. Her energy - vast, fresh, loving, nurturing and supportive, engulfed me instantly. She was going to help with the location and I was thrilled as I felt her take my hand.

I closed my eyes and saw a deep and ancient forest. The trees were mostly redwoods, but there were also smaller oaks and ashes, and lots of ferns and berries. As I looked around, I realized that Ramona would not feel safe waking up here. There were too many places where bad guys could hide. I took a few deep breaths of fresh forest air, thanked Gaia and requested a location with broad horizons instead.

The next location took me by surprise, it was a Caribbean beach, with sparkling white sand, a turquoise sea, scattered palm trees and low shrubs. The Horizon extended as far as the eye could see. The air was moist, but unlike the forest, it was also warm and smelled of the ocean. I looked down and felt the soft golden sand under my toes. Before I could request it, a small beach hut appeared. It had thin linen curtains for walls, and a large hammock in the middle.

This was perfect. It was an excellent location. It looked like the sun was about to come out. A tiny golden sliver appearing on the horizon, making the sea turn to millions of white sparkles. It appeared I was wearing a white summer dress and bare feet. I sat on the sand for a while feeling the warmth on my skin. It was so real that if I didn't already know it was a constructed reality, I would totally believe I was on a caribbean island somewhere. The energy of the guardian grew outwards from my body, encompassing the entire area as far as the eye could see. It also was a golden color. At least that's how my mind interpreted it.

I closed my constructed eyes and opened my physical eyes, then took Ramona's hand and felt for her consciousness. Not surprisingly, she was with Chad, and asleep.

Pulling them into the beach construct was not hard at all. I closed my physical eyes and was back in the beach hut. In front of me Ramona and Chad, suitably attired, lay on the hammock. The physical contact and the intent for them to join me was all that was needed.

"Ramona, wake up sleepy head," I whispered, "you are going to miss the sunrise."

Ramona struggled to open her eyes, looked around confused, "where are we?"

"Never mind that, come on, hurry, come see the sunrise."

She got up, wobbly, and I led her outside. We sat on the sand, and she kept nodding off as she squinted her eyes trying to watch the sun that now looked like half a bright white coin coming out of the deep sparkle filled ocean. The place bursting with life, fish in the water, birds taking flight, it was amazing.

"Ramona, I need you to see something else now."

She looked at me, I could feel that she was becoming fully conscious. I only had a few seconds.

I took both her hands and showed her the events of the last few hours. Including the meeting with the representatives from Alaster's species sub collectives.

Her eyes became two pits of darkness, her face morphed into some sort of beast, and she attacked.

I don't know the full details of what happened from her perspective exactly, but the short version is that she thought she had been tricked, that I was a bad guy, as was everyone else. She felt caged, which in a way she was, and that the only way out was through the complete destruction of her perceived enemies.

From my perspective, I suddenly was no longer 'me', Inelia Benz. I was something else. I was the entire landscape, the entire construct. I was every grain of sand, the air in our lungs, the palm trees, the ocean, the hut, Ramona, Chad and the constructed image and consciousness of Inelia Benz.

It felt like her strikes passed through the gap between atoms, her perception becoming stronger and broader, there was a split moment when she realized the nature of the construct we were in, felt Gaia, and she paused. That split moment pause was enough to interject the experience of being held to exist fully, to express and Be. No judgment, no rejection, no fighting back. Accompanied by an awareness for her to check for resonance of truth. An invitation to respond rather than react. I also reminded her of the reality where she was physically, sedated, still holding Chad's thumb with her pinky.

She took it. She was awake.

I opened my physical eyes, and watched Ramona come back into consciousness. Once she had become aware and awake in the

93

constructed reality, she was able to take back control of her body in the physical reality and bypass the sedative.

She pulled the IV feed off her hand and smiled, "you said they could fix Chad's brain damage?"

"Yes, well, I suggested they go ahead and do it. Not sure if they have yet or not."

"I guess we better find out, huh?" She said and took the IV off Chad's hand. Then placed her hands on his chest. He opened his eyes and gasped for air. Next, he looked deeply into Ramona's eyes, and then instantly wrapped her in his arms.

I stepped away. It seemed invasive to be there, during the moment they both saw each other again after so many years.

Alaster was waiting outside the room. There was an air of urgency about him, like he understood that time was needed, but that we didn't have any.

Strong forces surrounded the base, and it wasn't all energetic. There were people out there with guns too.

He nodded and took me outside of the building. I couldn't see anyone, but I could definitely feel them. It was similar to the feeling one gets when out on a hike and there's a large predator around such as a mountain lion or bear. Only this time, there was also a sharp energy of eliminating anyone who would stand in the way of their target.

I was really exhausted. I had lost track of time, but from my recollection, this morning was my second to last day in Costa Rica. I had not slept in 24 hours, was still being affected by the sedatives, found it hard to breathe, and the energy work with Ramona had taken its own toll.

Alaster could sense my exhaustion and said, "let's have breakfast. It will help."

I looked at him rather puzzled. Here we were being surrounded by bad guys, and Alaster wanted to go for breakfast. But then I realized

94

that there was nothing much I could do in my present state. As it was, I couldn't even think or see clearly. Breakfast was actually a good plan. The food would help clear the drugs from my body and give me some energy. We went back into the main building.

When we entered their staff cafeteria I was surprised to find that it looked like any other staff cafeteria around the world. But the food was fresh and full of lifeforce. I was also surprised to see that Alaster ate the same foods we did, as in 'us humans'.

Ramona and Chad were brought to us before we were finished and joined us for breakfast. There was a distinct change in Ramona's entire demeanor and energy. The only words I can use to describe it is 'complete'. Much of the anger and the defensiveness was gone. I'd never really met Chad, so I stood up and introduced myself. He shook my hand and we exchanged niceties.

It was a strange scene to have in the middle of what really was a battle of extraordinary proportions.

We sat and finished our breakfast while talking about the weather, local foods, and the benefits of daily non animal protein. It was kinda crazy.

I wanted to get to know Chad better, interview him too. But I knew that when this was done, I would never see him or Ramona again. So after we finished eating, I decided to ask him a few questions.

What I learned was that he was indeed a psychic assassin working for the other side. A better description for his role might be a light warrior, as 'assassin' is not a term they use to describe themselves with. And that he was indeed assigned by an agency, which might be described as the opposite of the agency Ramona worked for, to disable or eliminate her. A job he had not been able to complete because he had fallen hopelessly in love with her the moment he saw her.

It was strange to see these two people together. Her energy still felt like black transparent glass. Like the night sky, vast, and filled with stars. And his energy remained white as snow, and bright as the sun.

Like clear white glass, or looking into the brightest of snow covered landscapes on a sunny day. Yet here they were, side by side. Neither eliminating nor diminishing the beauty or intensity of the other. And I could sense the new field of energy that was both of them. It was so different that keeping it in my awareness or focus was nearly impossible. Almost like when we see something in the corner of our eye, but when we turn around to look at it, it's gone.

There was also something else. There was a sense of degrading quality to the edges of both their energy fields. Like their essences were being dissolved.

My own connection to what was happening around me was getting smaller and smaller. It was almost like I was becoming 'less' Inelia Benz. Less 'singular' and more something else. The Guardian energy was still in my field, was my field. But now there was something else too. It was like the holding of any type of construct, belief, reality, solidity, or desire for outcome, including my own person's existence, was quickly leaving me.

Alaster touched my arm and I heard his voice. I wondered why there had been a need for physical contact this time. There hadn't before.

"I, we, are also wondering what is happening to you. The best I can describe it, is almost like you are becoming this no man's land outside of time and space. It is not something we have ever seen before. And it's not just you, but carried across time and space by millions of human individuals. It is almost like by becoming aware of this location and its nature, the human collective is giving birth to it outside of time and space."

The funny thing is that when he said that, instead of becoming curious or wanting to expand on what he was seeing, like any regular person would, all I wondered was how would I recall his words as the mic could not pick them up from my head. The thought was so very funny at the time, I smiled.

Alaster responded, "we will make a recording and you can tap into it any time you need to."

I didn't exactly know how that was going to work, but I trusted that it would and my attention left the topic. As it happened, it feels like an extremely clear memory, almost like watching a 3D movie.

My main thought became: "how are we going to get these two out of here," referring to Ramona and Chad.

Then it came to me. The reason they were being affected by this place and why they had affected each other, disabled each other, was because of conscious or unconscious agreements. If they were to remove the agreement to be affected in any way by either side of the war between light and dark, then they could theoretically get out of here, live wherever they wanted and never be affected. The problem was that to achieve that level of clarity and empowerment could take years of work. Especially if a person was polarized in energy, like both Ramona and Chad were.

I felt a golden, bright energy expanding from my own physical body. It was the Guardian energy, but it was laced with something else. A very distinct quality. The only word that I can use to describe that other quality is "determined". It was an energy often described as stubbornness, but that is more accurately seen as a sure decision and complete follow through. Not always to good results or consequences, but that's not the point.

Both Ramona and Chad became aware of it. Chad smiled and Ramona frowned.

This was going to be interesting.

The energy of the Guardian moved through the space that divided us and started gently and slowly moving and engulfing Ramona and Chad. It appeared to be "asking" to become one with them.

Chad immediately said yes and he became golden and bright. Ramona watched Chad for a few minutes, feeling what he was feeling, then also said yes and she too became golden and bright.

I became aware that they were interpreting the look, color and feel of the energy to be different. But the result was the same. They were now the Guardian too.

"Well, this is unexpected," Ramona said, looking at her hands.

"It's the most amazing feeling," answered Chad. "It is like nothing can change my mind or remove me from being me."

The questions "who is doing this? Who is orchestrating this situation? Where did the Guardian energy come from?" Popped up in Alaster, Ramona, Chad and myself at the same instant.

"Not me." I quickly responded. "It feels like it's all of us."

And the moment I said those words, I knew that I didn't just mean the people in the room, but everyone who had ever existed.

"OK," that was Ramona, "so this Guardian shield thing is how we can minimize the energy attacks. Now we need to figure out how to deal with the flying bullets."

"Indeed," Alaster began, "they are outside our perimeter, so we cannot use our weapons on them."

Not that they would, even if they were inside, I thought.

Alaster looked at me and smiled.

"There are two things to take into consideration right now," I put in, "one is that we have to get Ramona and Chad out of here as soon as possible. I can see they are already being dissolved, for lack of a better word. The other thing we must consider is that after they are out of here, there has to be a way or a place, where they cannot be physically harmed. A place on our regular world, where their light and dark configurations can exist simultaneously as the new element is completely embodied."

When I said that, I felt a collective fear of the unknown. The fear hit me like a ton of bricks and I became aware that once that fear was processed, things would change radically.

"Ramona, Chad, can you see the new element you are becoming?"

They both looked at each other for a few moments, then nodded.

"You need to allow any fear you may have about it to exist, grow and express itself. Do you think you can do that?"

"Yes." The answer was unanimous. I was surprised that it also came from Alaster and his collective consciousness. That they would be afraid of this new element had not crossed my mind.

I closed my eyes and felt deeply into my core essence to see if I was personally afraid of the new element. The answer was also yes. That surprised me too.

Simply looking at this fear, was enough to start dissolving it.

"Do you guys know how to place ideas, experiences, energies and thoughts into the minds of others that will appear to be their own?" I was asking Ramona and Chad. I knew that Alaster could, and that he would not do it in this instance.

"Yes," Ramona said, and looked at Chad. I'd forgotten that she had never realized that Chad was as powerful a mystic as she was.

"Yes," Chad answered.

"OK. So, this is what I'm thinking. We create an amplified projection, by joining our skills. And after that, you two embody the new element as much as you can in your emotions, thoughts and interpretations, and send it to everyone out there. Every member of both agencies. Project it to anyone and everyone on the planet who wants to feel it, be it, for a moment. That they can take it or leave it, but out of their own free will. What do you think?"

"I don't see the point," said Chad.

"It's how one stops being afraid and can step into making a decision based on true self and information rather than egoic constructs or agendas," responded Ramona. "It's what happened to me on the Caribbean island."

"What Caribbean island?" Asked Chad.

"I'll tell you all about it later." She responded.

"Yes, basically when something is no longer an unknown, we are more likely to not want to destroy it or stop it. We are much more likely to allow it to exist and expand." I added, "there are no guarantees that it will work as some people might still choose that they want to eliminate, use, exploit, or own the element, but at least most of the fear and negativity about it will be removed from their decision. It enhances good decision making to make the unknown known."

"Sounds good to me. I'm game." Said Chad.

"We could interject the decision to let it exist, let us exist in peace and leave us alone," said Ramona.

"Well, that would violate their free will. Everyone knows when their free will is being violated, even if at a very unconscious level, and will respond very negatively to that happening. It would backfire on us." I said.

I could have gone on to explain to her, that telling people what to do or what decisions to make was not something I was capable of, or willing to do. It is a complete contradiction to raising the vibration of the planet as well as the opposite of what empowerment means. But I felt it was neither necessary nor relevant at this point.

"We would like to provide you with a suitable location for you to carry this exercise out," said Alaster, standing up and gesturing to the door.

Chapter Nine: Freedom

I was expecting Alaster to take us into a nice quiet room. With cushions on the floor perhaps, or very comfy chairs. Where he actually took us was way more amazing than I could possibly have imagined.

The base we were in was just a small external entryway into a seemingly huge underground compound of rooms, some of them huge, with tunnels leading off into the distance.

We took what could be best described as a speed elevator with seats, but it appeared to move sideways and up and down as well as front and back at different points.

When the elevator doors opened, all three of us, Ramona, Chad and I, gasped in amazement and awe.

The "room" looked like it was outdoors, on the surface. But I could sense it wasn't. The sky looked like real sky, and as we stepped out of the elevator, a few rays of sunshine touched my skin as they came through the greenest canopy of trees I had ever seen. The leaves were that bright, fresh green of spring newborn life.

The air smelled fresh, faintly of orange blossoms. Past the trees, there was a lake. Its waters were crystal clear, vast and pure. Bordering the lake was the forest, hills and in the distance, mountains.

"I don't understand," I said, referring to the fact that we were underground but by all evidence, we had to be outside, above ground.

Alaster responded, "most of you have been taught that what you see from your eyes, and all your other senses, is what is coming from outside of yourself. That it is real, and that it is solid, and that it is you who move and walk around within it. That the environment is an external thing."

He picked up some stones and handed one each to us, "you also believe that what you perceive as real, as your environment, is not corrupted or changed by yourself or others. That it is separate from you, and that it is also independent from you. The reality you live in is that the world, Earth, is round, that it has an atmosphere, it's made of rocks and water, and that you live on its surface. But have you never thought that perhaps that reality is truly a convenient projection of your own minds? Of your own collective consciousness?"

"Are you saying that the world is not round and that we don't live on its surface?" Ramona asked.

"I am saying that it is one perception and interpretation of where you live."

"So, what is your interpretation?" she said.

"My interpretation, our interpretation, is that the world, our world, is not round. And that it does not have an outside or an inside."

"Escher's Relativity." I said, remembering a drawing by M. C. Escher. The drawing depicted a room that had many ceilings, floors and stairs going into different spaces, both up and down, and upside up down, simultaneously.

"Yes," Alaster responded, "and as in his painting called 'Drawing Hands', the environment and its creator are not really separate.

I didn't fully grasp the enormity of what he was expressing, but I understood the basic idea. "So we really are at the surface of the planet, but also underground."

"Yes."

"So, the splitting of the light and dark duality on Earth right now, I mean human Earth, might just be a splitting of the physical perception of what Earth is by those who choose empowerment from those who choose fear?" I asked.

"Yes, one could say that the majority of 'Earths' came about through splits in reality constructs, agreements and perception by one or more species. It's one Earth though."

I had to stop for a moment to think about this, "if there is only one Earth, that means there's one Gaia. But for a while now I have perceived that Gaia chose to be at a higher vibration of existence, that she is in fact living at a very high vibrational, empowered level and is simply waiting for us, the ones who are choosing empowerment, to catch up with her. But if what you are saying is that the split happens in Gaia herself, then that perception is not accurate. It would mean she has also chosen a very dark, power over others continuation of the old paradigm." I wanted to expand more on the idea, but couldn't really find the words.

Alaster did seem to know what I was talking about and responded, "the only way I understand it, is that she is not one short, small spectrum of vibration, but a huge spectrum. That she is fully conscious of the entire spectrum. That each band of vibration exists within its own time and space, like the cells in a body. Or the trees in an Aspen forest. When a person chooses one or the other band of vibration, they perceive it in Gaia and get pulled there. That's why some people see a completely destroyed, polluted, devastated, raped Gaia, that needs saving, and others see a powerful, empowered, amazingly bright, high vibrational Gaia that is waiting. It's not that one denies or invalidates the other, it's just like two different cells in a body or two trees in the same forest. And that humans as relatively narrowly focused physical beings perceive only the cell or tree they live in, or are moving into. There are some species which dedicate themselves to the exploration of "Earths", or bands of vibrational perception. Fascinating people."

I had a million other questions. But time was short. I could always ask more later, after we were done. After the danger was over.

"What a trip." Said Ramona, touching the nearest tree.

"There is a lovely sitting area about five minutes from here," said Alaster as he started walking.

My mind was racing a thousand miles an hour. Just when it seemed that reality could not become stranger, it did. I took a few deep breaths and started looking at the layout of the landscape. The direction we were walking led to a perfect geometrical spot that crossed energy lines from the lake, the nearest hills, mountains and the forest itself.

Following resonance and moving away from dissonance, we chose a spot very close to the water.

The three of us sat down on the ground and Alaster walked back to where we had come from, disappearing into the forest.

We didn't say anything, we didn't have to. We sat down without a thought. They were facing each other, their knees almost touching. I was facing them a few yards away. The word "witness" came to mind. This was so cool, they would do this without my participation. I would simply witness, creating a door into the new element for anyone who wanted to explore it, enter it, or simply observe it after I wrote the book.

The steps were clear... we would create a broadcast link that went directly into people's minds, whether conscious or unconscious. Once that link was in place, Ramona and Chad would simply step into and embody the new element and everything they felt, experienced and were, would be transmitted directly into the human collective. Perhaps even into the collective of every species on the planet and those beyond.

They nodded to me, they were ready.

I closed my eyes and felt the broadcast link appear. It spread quickly across, around, and through the world. Billions of voices, experiences, lives appeared in my mind. And it was done. We were broadcasting live and clear.

Suddenly I felt the new element as a part of me, as part of my mind, my entire being. The energy, the very existence of it cracked into my awareness like a thunderbolt. I could sense it spreading around the planet, into every voice, every experience, every mind. It had become like a wave rippling outwards, quickly and cleanly.

There was a pause in the collective mind, the noise stopped for a millisecond and it felt like it was listening. Then the noise began again. This time there was curiosity, fear, anger, familiarity. Then that faded, and the noise returned.

And then the new element came back towards us. It retreated back from all directions as fast as it had expanded. It felt like what a large flowing river might feel like if all the water was to pass right through our bodies. And then it stopped.

I opened my eyes and saw a ball of light of the most beautiful and indescribable color. It was hovering exactly between Ramona and Chad. They were looking into each other's eyes, and smiling. It was the most amazingly beautiful light I had ever seen in my life. As I observed it, it felt as though it was pulling me in, like the light became everything, everywhere, throughout time and space. I felt my consciousness disappear into it. Then out. I was back to observing the light from my own body.

Suddenly it expanded, covering both of them, and then it vanished... and with it went Chad and Ramona. They were gone.

I gasped.

I quickly scanned the area. There was no sign of them, not a trace. Ramona and Chad, and the new element, were gone. All that was left was the guardian energy. It was all around, part of every leaf, mountain and rock. It was the lake and the sky, the birds, and the air. Then even this energy started becoming less and less perceivable.

I stayed quietly watching as the guardian energy started to dissipate. Dissolving, becoming other energies and vibrations all around me. And then it too was gone.

My heart was beating hard. I remembered to breathe again and just sat there waiting. I'm not exactly sure what I was waiting for, but I had no perception or wish to do anything else.

At some point Alaster arrived and sat next to me.

An eternity later I asked, "what happened to them?" Not sure if he knew any better than I did, but it was worth asking.

"Genesis happened." He said.

I looked over at him, not fully grasping what he was saying.

"Across worlds, and across cultures in each world, there are stories of the origin of man. The great majority have the original man and original woman arriving from the sky, or created by God, and that's when history begins. That's when the world starts."

"Ramona and Chad? The Adam and Eve of a new world?"

"Yes."

"But, those stories don't make sense. How can one man and one woman give birth to an entire planet filled with people?"

"They don't. They simply leave the door open for people to come in to the new expression and perception of Gaia. They leave the door open to the new cell in her body, the new tree in the forest."

"First there was nothing, then there was Ramona and Chad. From whom an entire planet was born." I said, "I can see how that could easily be misinterpreted."

Alaster smiled, "the main misinterpretations are simply that it is often believed to be the only planet, or a solidly round planet where no one else exists anywhere else or any other time."

"But it's just a different spectrum of perception occupying probably the same time space." I said.

"Maybe."

"There was a split in the human collective, a few years ago. Our species went into two different directions. One was into empowerment and expanded awareness, the other into further power over others and disempowerment. As I look at the new Earth, the new color of reality that Ramona and Chad gave birth to, I'm thinking that there is a third option available now."

It was as I said those last words, that I realized that there were more than those three options available to us now. The fact that Alaster and his people had become visible to us, publicly visible, meant that their reality, their Earth, where light and dark did not exist, was also open for us to experience and step into if we so wished.

Alaster nodded and added, "all an individual needs to do is see the Earth as she really is, and reality, and whatever life experience they want to have, is open to them. There are as many Earth expressions as there are people to dream them."

I sighed and stood up, stretching my legs.

"We'll arrange transport back to your hotel and airport. Your flight leaves in a few hours." He said.

"My flight back home." I thought. He nodded.

Somehow what was home was so irrelevant right now, that it felt like that was the illusion, a dream dreamed and finished long ago.

"What will you do?" Asked Alaster. He meant about the book. Would I publish it? Would I shelve it?

But the answer was already clear. It was clear because across time and space the new element was known, perceived and an option for anyone to enter into that reality using whatever belief system allowed them to move through Gaia's cell walls or tree roots, or whatever way we explain the stairs between up and down which are down and up. Death and rebirth, portals around the planet, places like these, no man's lands. All were possible paths to the new world. To any of the alternative worlds.

"I am going home and I'm going to write it." I said, "then I might publish it."

Leaving the compound in the black car, I watched as men moved through the trees. Some red laser lights flashed into my eyes, and on the glass... I could see them aimed at my chest and head. It was unclear what they would do at first, but after a few minutes, it became clear that I had safe passage. I exhaled a sigh of relief and closed my eyes. It felt like I hadn't slept for days and the trip back to the hotel was a long one.

"Would you like a pillow madam?" It was one of the big bulky men sitting next to me.

"Yes, that would be lovely, thank you."

Postscript

On my way home, on the flight, I felt for the new element in our collective, but I could not find it. All I could find was a slight awareness. A small feeling, an energy that was on the edges of joy and excitement. Like the dream of a beautiful landscape that is barely visible.

But I knew it would spread.

Even though I could not, and would not be able to describe it for many years, simply being aware that it existed, that every person who would read this book to this page would be aware of it, would make it more real, more available, more describable. At some point in the future we would know of it by name, by experience, and it will have reality, and probably a history, mythology, and even artifacts in our own reality. At that point the memory of it before it existed would only be recalled by books like this one.

When I got home, there was an envelope stuck to my door. Inside, four words:

"Dear Friend,

Thank you."

I opened the door and stepped inside. My dog came running and I heard the voices of my loved ones coming to greet me. After a few hours of hugs, stories and updates, I walked into my study and switched on my computer.

I typed:

INTERVIEW WITH A PSYCHIC ASSASSIN

a novel by Inelia Benz

20534369R00073

Made in the USA
San Bernardino, CA
14 April 2015